Magona's Rise

Book 2

By Lucas Brady

Hardcover: 979-8-9867076-3-1
Paperback: 979-8-9867076-2-4

First hardcover edition August 2022

Written by Lucas Brady
Edited by Lucas Brady
Cover photography Copyright © 2022 Lucas Brady

Printed by KDP Print in the USA

Kindle Direct Publishing
410 Terry Ave N
Seattle, WA 98109

This book is dedicated to Jane Gentry and Alexander Lee

TABLE OF CONTENTS

~The Messages....5

~The Creation....6

~The Follower....10

~The Ace....33

~The Arthropodians....57

~The Ball....71

~The Mistake....82

~The Auction....106

~The History....122

~The Eye....139

~The Castle....152

~The Al-X....170

~The Station....195

~The Note....203

~The Seventh....206

~The Creature Log....220

~The Order of The Universe....234

~The Messages~

"As the person Janx is inspired by, I wanted to say thank you for purchasing Loca. Lots of time and effort was poured into this book by myself, and especially the author, Lucas. I am forever grateful to be a part of this project. <3"

-Jane Gentry (Janx)

"(Al-X) is this big fat oil baron who controls a whole planet as his empire. The only thing we have in common is that we're fat and greasy. I don't get paid enough for being in this book."

-Alexander Lee (Al-X)

"I'm really happy I was able to get featured in a full-length book. I'm even happier that I'm getting paid...Wait, I'm not getting paid? Oh, never mind."

-Dominick Necastro (Dhamaneek)

~The Creation~

The area around me begins. It's created as I am. I have no body… I'm just energy; I can feel nothing besides my thoughts. I think about being able to do anything, and I'm given a body. I'm not sure what I did to receive it, but I'm grateful. I have hands that can touch and legs that can move. I use them to my advantage.

I walk around the nothing around me and use my fingers to twirl the heat and matter that floats throughout. They mix and collide until an outburst of color shines through. The empty space is now colorful.
Another creature pops into existence, one with yellow skin and more light. He runs around the space I created, a little ball of light being made with each step he takes. Some of these balls are immensely large, so I decide to wipe the heat off. What's left is a giant orb of possibility, so I feel the presence of another.

A creature of white sticks melded together fades above the planet I hold. It rubs its hands around the world, and little creatures rise from the dirt. They run around, some attacking each other and others simply relaxing. However, a few creations stop moving, and a smaller skeleton appears to take them away.

A flabby man appears, his skin bouncing as he trudges through the space to send some dust onto the creatures. They begin to do more things, like connect with others and form bonds. One of the animals grows into a being like us, which helps overlook the bonds between all creatures.

One of the races made was by a sixth being. He makes a specific kind of creation that he made sure to be perfect. He proves to be very special since the creatures develop very advanced thought patterns.

One last being is brought into our reality, and he doesn't do anything. He hangs around us, not knowing I don't want him. But, as I watch over this virgin universe, I witness his fall into love with another race; a god with the appearance of a Sporetrop intertwining with a measly mortal Kuroledy, a species of pale white skin, the blackest hair, but the brightest pink eyes.

They should not be together. Only Gellax can create new breeds; it is not the job of the universe's inhabitants to do so. If this…cross-race breeding does happen, I must be the one to reverse it. I cannot do it alone…I must sneakily coerce my fellow rulers to help me on my journey, but how?

Perhaps we could craft a weapon that could tap into Gellax's energy…and have all disobeyers become one with space; to make a graveyard of sinners. Their energy and souls could be repurposed into true lifeforms. And if this…weapon is created, then that bubbly Kuroledy shall be the first to taste its freedom.

—

"Nobody will believe you," I say to The Seventh as he holds the fading corpse of his Kuroledy partner in his arms. He screams for my name, but I block his voice out.

The sand-colored brick chamber around us echoes with the screams of the Kuroledy. The first step is done; the sword is functional, and now I shall bring everyone to this beautiful planet I call Roan. Then the conversion will begin.

I drop the blade onto the ground, letting The Seventh have an opportunity to strike me down with it. I know he wants to. I hear his scurrying behind me, and the feeling of a slash burns into my popliteal fossae. I stand still and smile with my back to The Seventh as my body slowly vanishes, and I feel my soul merge with the energy around me. I find myself in a world similar to the physical one. I see sound waves moving around me and mortals' auras running past. I have done it.

—

I step onto the slushy dirt of a bog. Curving light brown trees rise from the patches of shallow ponds. The lime grass brushes against my cloaked legs as I walk through. In the distance, I can see green mountains dotted with trees as the soft kiss of the wind touches my pulsing forehead. My fellow true-race followers accompany my travels, walking behind me with their hooded black robes blending with their shadows. Lord Daytör stands by my left side, his white mask reflecting the harsh yellow light of the sun above.

"Do you have it?" I ask him. He nods, pulling his right sleeve and tapping on a shard of bent metal across his robotic humerus. "Find me that last piece…and we shall revert this universe back into the pure one Gellax began."

"Yes, my lord," Daytör says. He rallies up some followers, and they begin to move in all directions as I kneel onto the overgrown land. My eyes close, and I feel the blades of green wrap around my legs, pulling me down. I let my body blend with the dirt, and a spread of blackness envelops the area around me. The bog above becomes a hellscape; dark clouds, pits of molten lava, and a forever rain of ash.

In my mind's eye, I can see this planet of Loca being the perfect shell for my plan. But as I fantasize, a body materializes in my vision. A blank face, yet one with a million features; a body of pure energy. If I could only find them…I feel a connection like I've seen them before. Its mouth moves, speaking in silence, and my mind's eye shatters like glass. The pieces rattle around my empty shell of a skull as I feel another connection course through my veins.

~The Follower~

I wake up to the bright yellow light of the sun in my room and the sound of knocking on my door. I sit in my bed for a moment, with my messy hair covering my eyes. I brush it back as another set of knocking comes from my door. I set my feet on the floor and search for my slippers. I bend down to check under the bed, but only boxes are underneath. I groan as I get back up and walk to the door next to the large white fridge in the kitchen. I unlock the door's sliding locks and open it wide.

"Hello! I just moved in next to you and was wondering if I could stop by and say hi!" a voice says as soon as I open the door. I look out into the hallway to see a female Arachnavoid. Spider-human hybrids that are as tall as ordinary people, with six arms, two legs, two large eyes, six small eyes, and the characteristics of a normal arachnid. This one is a bit different.

This Arachnavoid has two bulbous dark red eyes and six smaller eyes above them; three over each large eye. The middle of each eye has a smudgy lighter red pupil that follows your movements. Her skin is a light gray, with the usual small layer of hairs that move independently. And just like usual, six spiny arms on the side, two smaller arms in front, and two legs. Her mouth is the normal Arachnavoid, too, with a small circular opening with a sharp fang on either side.

The different part is with her hair; Arachnavoids can grow human-like hair on the face or the head. The hair is typically straight and either simple black or brown. This one has curly brown hair with blonde highlights. Also, this Arachnavoid is wearing dirty black overalls and tar-covered white sneakers.

She looks around the hallway, then rushes into my apartment and closes the door behind her. She puts her body against the door, panting from the run-in.

"My name is Arachcait, and I'm being followed," she says.

—

I look out into the golden-wallpapered, smelly hallway, peeking only my head out of the door. After confirming nobody is around, I lock it up. I rest my head on the door and groan.

Who is this? Why am I trusting her? This could be someone trying to kill ME.

I take a quick breath and swiftly turn around to face Arachcait sitting on the couch, holding herself with all six arms. She has a worried expression on her face, with all eight of her eyes staring at the ground. She moves her legs to the right, sinking into the dusty cushions. The smell of dew has stunk the air ever since she entered. I walk into the kitchen and take out a cold mug from the freezer. My personal favorite and only mug I own is the black one with the logo for the Austomplinor's Guns and Grub gun shop.

I set it on the small counter and grab a coffee maker from one of the shelves. Then, I grab the Coffee Mill Grind-R, a small, rectangular device that turns coffee beans into a liquid that can be poured into a cup. Then, I grab a bag of coffee beans from a shelf under the counter, picking the yellow Brench Coast variety, named after a beautiful scenic location near the edge of the Province of Stoean. Then, I dump the entire bag into the top of the coffee maker; then, the beans magically melt into a soupy, yellow-brown liquid. I pour the liquid into the mug, then stir it with my finger.

"You thirsty?" I ask Arachcait.

She doesn't turn around or respond. Instead, she only stares out of the window to the early morning bustling town. Creatures of different species move from place to place, always going somewhere but never arriving. I walk next to the couch, looking at her side profile. Arachcait's dark red eyes seem lighter than usual. It could be because of the sunlight, but I think it's caused by fluids being released, like tears or sweat.

I think about that being a possibility, but the apparent fact that Arachnavoids do not possess tear ducts shoots down my idea. I grab one of the pillows and flip it on its side. Arachcait moves her eyes towards me, but not her head. I pat the pillow flat and then set the mug onto it.

"Please give me a different answer. Who's following you?" I ask, this being my fifth time.

"I told you already, the big man!" Arachcait yells from under her breath. Her eyes shake as she stares at me. I angrily close my eyes and sigh.

"Who is the big man? I've asked you this a million times. I just want to know."

"All I need is to stay here until he picks a new one," Arachcait says, returning to her relaxed state.

She's been avoiding the question for an hour now. She ran in, hid behind the couch for ten minutes, then sat biting her fingers. I don't know who the big man is or what he's picking.

I walk into my bedroom and over to the skinny closet. I am very slim anyway, and I can't even fit in the closet. All that's hanging up is a few corsets, some black jeans and leggings, a few mismatched pairs of black socks, and some other miscellaneous clothing. Some shoes are on the closet floor, such as my tall black boots, black heels, and black running sneakers. I grab the broken corset from my bed and crack it back into place, although it doesn't fix completely. I hold a long black t-shirt from a hanger and swap it for the corset. I throw on the t-shirt and ruffle my hair until it's less like a rat's nest.

I close the bedroom door and quickly remove my leggings. Covering my legs are plenty of scars and cuts. Bandages or tissues cover most, but some are still open wounds that hurt when I touch them. I see one new cut, about a finger long, above my left knee. I sigh as I drop to my ass on the edge of my bed. The wound is fresh since it's still leaking a tiny bit of blood. I attempt to wipe it, but it smears the blood across my thigh.

"Fuck," I whisper to myself. I waste too much of my hard-earned sugola coins on medical products. Every time I go out on a job, I return to my apartment covered in new cuts and probably sporting a few fatal problems. I stand up onto my scarred legs and grab a pair of black jeans from my closet. I put one leg in, the other, then button the front. I open the bedroom door to see Arachcait downing the coffee. She holds the mug upside down over her mouth so every drop lands.

"Like the coffee?" I call out. She jumps and drops the mug, which shatters into pieces as it collides with the hardwood floor. I'm disappointed for a moment, but I ask again.

"Yes," her soft yet raspy voice responds. I nod and walk back into my room. I open my map to see a new marker in a random location, on the other side of Loca from where I am. The closest civilization to the marker is the City of Leath. I close and open the map back up, but the marker stays in its far-off spot. I raise an eyebrow as I zoom in—the map switches from 3D to a 2D bird's eye view.

The ground map shows a large clearing, miles in size, surrounded by a small layer of trees. I think I should ignore it as a notification pops up. Next mission, Janx. Files are under your door. When I finish reading the short message, I run out of the room to see Arachcait standing at the door, looking down at the folder on the ground. It's a folder like before, with a detailed paper and a paperclipped photo.

This time, the photo is a mugshot of a Mushrumian, a native mushroom-headed species. They live in the caves of Mushrumia, near the Province of Stoean's mining colony. Their bodies are usually featureless, white or gray blobs that they hop around on, and their heads are large mushroom tops with varying patterns. They do not have eyes, so they use vibrations to see. They do have mouths but communicate only in the ancient Mushrumian language.

This Mushrumian's name is Lepio-N Brunne, and his pattern is a bone-like transparent white. Faint Mushrumian language etchings can be made out in the photo, but the exact words cannot be translated. I don't read the paper beside the crime list, which I have never done before. The list reads Armed robbery, assault, murder, and torture.

There is a reason I do not read about the people I kill. Each person I am tasked with killing should be judged by whoever waits for them on the other side. Not by me. I should not be the one to decide how someone dies; I only kill them however I can at that moment. Reading part of Lepio-N's file makes me sick. I close the file, throwing it onto the kitchen counter.

"What's that?" Arachcait asks, quivering in her arms. I turn my head until I can see her from the corner of my eye. My lips lower. I open them to speak, but nothing comes out. "Who are you? A lawyer?"

"No, I...," I start, turning my head away from her.

Do I tell her? She feels safe from...whoever the 'big man' is.

"Listen," I continue. "I kill for rewards. But I only kill bad Locanagwans. I don't discriminate on anything besides what they've done. So don't worry, you're safe with me. If the big man comes for you, I can kill him."

"Really?" Arachcait asks. I can tell she's still scared but has gained some trust back. I turn my head until she can see my face, and then I slowly nod. My lips raise—a smile forms. Neither of us speak for a few moments, but looking in Arachcait's eyes, I can tell exactly what she's thinking. When stressed and worried, her eyes would slightly shake while stationary. But now they remain still.

"Well, with that information out now, I need to do this next job." I walk over to the counter and open the folder back up. "This shouldn't take too long; it's just some mushroom creature. I'll pick up some more food when I get back."

Arachcait nods and returns to the couch, laying on it with her head smashed into a pillow. I walk into the bedroom and take off my t-shirt. I notice a rip in the left sleeve, which I ignore. I retrieve one of my many corsets, ensuring my pockets are full of what I need. I put it on and button it up.

As I walk towards the door, I notice Arachcait has passed out on the couch. I pause for a second, then walk over to her. Then, I kneel and pet her arm, dangling off the couch.

It's slightly fuzzy, almost like a deer hide.

After two arm-length pets, I return to the door. I turn the knob and walk out into the lightless hallway. I look toward either end of the hallway, seeing yards of white wooden doors on each side. Straight from my apartment door is the elevator. I press the down button on the right of the elevator, and it opens immediately. The claustrophobic, blinding white metal walls of the elevator are frightening to most newcomers, but I'm used to it. I usually squint my eyes while riding it.

I walk in and press the lobby floor on the button panel. The double metal doors close with a thud, which shakes the elevator. I stand undisturbed. It begins to move downward at a snail's pace, and I stand at the back right, leaning against the wall. The elevator music starts playing, and it sounds like a piano. It distorts at random moments but is relaxing, to say the least. Above the doors is a screen that displays the elevator's location, and as it passes the second floor, I push myself off the wall. I walk in front of the door, and as the elevator slows down, I prepare to speed walk out.

The shake of the elevator reaching the end moves me, but only enough for my left foot to scoot an inch forward. The doors begin opening as I rush out, bumping into someone walking in. I turn around to apologize and see two large Zargons in black suits with their backs to me, black suits that are surprisingly shiny. One has orange scales while the other has purple. They both have the long, curved back horns Zargons are known for. They enter the elevator, and it closes without them pressing anything.

What was their deal? They must be new; I've never seen Zargons live here before.

I quickly dismiss them, walking through the empty lobby. Empty of people, of course, but not empty of decoration. The lobby is a yard or two wide, with two water fountains on either side. The walls have a newly painted over piss colored wallpaper, with a black metal trim. Oddly enough, the lobby is bare of any windows, and the reception desk is on the first floor instead of here.

I walk over the green carpet floor through the revolving glass door into the darkness outside. Outside of the apartment complex is a single road that leads into town. Besides that, the surrounding area is just a bunch of flat grass and few trees. It always smells like freshly trimmed grass in the morning, and then the night brings a new smell every afternoon. Tonight smells like oil.

Mushrumia is far away, and I know only one quick way to travel; the Lükahmp Train. It's only a few blocks past the nightclub, so I won't take long walking to it.

—

After walking past the decently built houses, and the nightclub, I walk through the shining glass doors to the Lükahmp Train Station. The station itself is pretty big. It's around three hundred feet wide and one hundred and fifty feet deep. The station's ceiling has a large window dome, and I can see the beginning of a storm brewing. The ground is full of rows upon rows of gray wooden benches and, of course, the train itself, in the middle of the station.

A train with fifteen-passenger cars, each twenty-five feet long; The front car and the caboose are both twenty-eight feet long. Decorated with a black exterior, the train can blend in with the night. Each car has about five dirty windows on each side and is filled with cushioned leather seats on either side. You don't need a ticket to get on—just yourself.

As I approach the empty middle section, I see two black-suited Zargons like before on the other side of the platform. They look the same as before, but with bloody knuckles. I act like I don't see them, and the train rushes in with a thunderous screech. The wind blows my hair back, and I close my eyes for a moment.

After a few seconds, the train stops with an elongated crash sound, and the breeze quiets down. I fix my hair and open my eyes, trying to peek in between the train cars for the Zargons. Then, straining my neck to the side, I see nothing. I try to move to the side, but I am pushed inside by the oncoming riders. I fall onto one of the seats, hitting my spine against the wall. I cringe in pain but act as if nothing happened.

The passengers all fill up the seats, with some standing. I can make out a few humans, a few cyborgs, and even a fellow assassin. Her name is Liqweel, and she wears the armor of the fallen knight, Mondio Sulez, who fought in the Battle of Stoean a few years ago. The armor includes a metal chest plate painted with dried blood of varying colors and a cylindrical helmet with two holes for eyes, bars over the mouth, and Zargon-like horns on either side. After exchanging a wave with Liqweel, I rest my hands on my lap and rest my eyes.

—

The train comes to a halt, knocking people over onto the cold floor. I awake as I crash against one of the seats, the rugged cushions cracking into my jaw. Mumors and whispers start growing louder as I peek through one of the windows into the pouring rain. All I can see is the dark grass and drops of water flicking the glass. Some of the train doors open, and the lights shut off, leaving us in darkness.

I climb back to my feet, peering out into the outside again. This time, I see something. A figure covered in a black cloak. He has a small plate on his chest, with two tubes feeding into the black of his hood. Behind him, creatures come out from the darkness, almost like the void is birthing them. They are all tall, light gray figures with abnormal body proportions.

Once they walk into the moonlight, I can tell they are Garabeshers, just like the thing I fought in that bunker. Human-like figures with deep black eyes, forever open mouths, zombie-like patches of hair, and drained skin. They vary in size amongst themselves but are much taller than humans. Their limbs are long, with their fingers dragging along the ground when they walk. Legends from schoolchildren in the Province of Carishem tell of Garabeshers hiding amongst trees in the schools' forests. They would stalk prey and consume the flesh of the alone.

What are they doing here, commanded by someone? They are usually on their own. And was that one in the bunker sent by this guy? Is Julia-N somewhere on this train?

The man in the cloak stops just inches away from the car door as he lifts his arms. The sleeves drop down to reveal robotic arms and hands, each joint being a separate piece, all connected by loose wires. Both arms have loose wiring and cracks in the metal, exposing the internal bits. He slowly raises his arms to his hood, pulling it down behind his head. A mask reveals itself, shining in the light and looking down at the muddy ground.

A long, skinny white mask, with two red lines on either side stretching from the forehead to the bottom of the nose. Where the mouth should be are two tall slits, with visible air breathing out of them. I can see the end of the two tubes going into his cheek area. Patches of dirt and scratch marks sparkle in the moonlit rain. He raises his head, looking directly at the train, letting more of his face light up. One wide but short gash in the middle of the mask makes itself known and shows gray skin and black eyes with small red pupils.

He lowers his arms and pulls up the sleeve on his left arm. The rain clinks against his exposed metal. He rams his right hand through a crack on his left arm, peeling back the material to reveal some tiny metal object lying inside. He pulls it out, and it burns a bright orange through the moonlight. I can tell it is half of Magona's Sword.

A sword that many people believe to be the end of free will, it was forged by the seven ancient gods of the universe. After a discourse on who should wield it, the blade was broken into ten pieces, scattered throughout the galaxy. This man has nine, only missing the sharp end. The sword is made of pure hell lava, with a forever glowing orange blade. The hilt is woven from the fabric of the sheep of Loca's second moon, Trakopre.

"I have tracked you throughout the moons of Loca and found you on this train. Make yourself known, traitor," the man speaks in a deep, robotic voice. Everyone on the train shrinks down in fear. "I will give you one minute to surrender yourself, or we board this train and take it by force."

Everyone begins to scream and freak out, trying to exit the other side of the train. I stay positioned where I am, looking for anyone suspicious. I look to my left, seeing nothing but people yelling for their lives. I turn to the right, seeing the same thing and Liqweel. Then, without taking her eyes off the window, she pulls a knife from under her chest plate and cuts one of the doors open. I turn my head and see a faint orange glow from her left pocket.

"Liqweel!" I call out. She turns at me, letting her guard down as the glass in front of her shatters from a bullet passing through. She turns her head back to the cloaked man, but the bullet passes through her helmet, splattering brain matter onto the opposite window. Her body falls onto the ground with a hard thud. My eyes bolt everywhere, with my mind racing.

What the hell is happening? I thought Liqweel was just an assassin, not a thief. Should I take that shard? If he gets it, he might enslave everyone or kill us.

After Liqweel's body falls, everyone screams louder and begins to break through the windows. Then, through the chaos, I run over to her body and take the shard out with my pointer and thumb, hiding it inside my corset pockets. I lift myself out of one of the broken windows and join the other passengers fleeing. Before I can get too far, I overhear them.

"This is her?... Then where is the piece?... Someone stole it?... Where did you see that, huh?... Pathetic," the cloaked man says, obviously to his minions. I turn my head towards the oncoming darkness as I think about where to go next.

—

I must have been out for a few hours. The train made it closer to Mushrumia than I thought. The fleeing group and I make it to the gates of Stoean after running through the rain for what felt like ages. My clothes are soaked; my hair sticks to the back of my neck. The cloaked man must not have suspected anyone else because we quickly got away from him.

I enter through the gates to Stoean, which are just two large, ten-foot-tall metal doors that are only there for decoration. But, unlike Carishem, the Province of Stoean welcomes its visitors.

—

A history lesson about the Province of Stoean. One of the oldest cities in Loca but also one of the smallest. It's made up of houses made of wood, stone, or any material builders could get their hands on. Each home is supported by a few feet of wooden planks since it's on the edge of an ocean. Near the beach is the Brench Coast, a factory-turned restaurant that used to house hundreds of families daily, now damaging the environment with its oil spills.

Building on what I said earlier, Carishem is the opposite of Stoean. While the Province of Carishem is a corrupt, slimy town full of gamblers and soulless workers, Stoean is a city ruled with order. Everyone wants to live here, even if the house prices are outrageously high. Every time I enter Stoean, everyone has a smile on their face and greets me, unaware that I'm always there to off someone.

Near the beautiful green sand beaches of Stoean are the unpleasant mining colonies. Looking for the rarest and most valuable materials, workers mine for hours, contracting deadly diseases that make parts of the underground biohazardous.

Now, my mission is to kill Lepio-N, who lives in Mushrumia, near the Stoean mining colony. Yet, my map marker shows him miles away, near the treacherous City of Leath. It's a good thing I escaped death and found myself near Stoean since I can get some answers on where Lepio-N is if this marker is to be believed.

—

"Where is Lepio-N, sir," I ask one of the Mushrumians in their ancient tongue. I have just made it through the mining tunnels to the small caves of Mushrumia. You know you made it when the cavern walls are covered in baby Mushrumians. About five babies are produced every few weeks, and Mushrumians usually live to be around thirty years.

"He left a while ago, said he was being followed," a Mushrumian with a green striped top responds to me while taking one of the babies out from the wall with its mind.

"Did he say where?" I ask. The Mushrumian holds the child in the air as it begins to take out another child next to it. Both children have blank tops. Designs aren't genetic; they are painted on after Mushrumians achieve adulthood.

"City of Leath," I slowly shake my head as I hear him confirm my thoughts.

"Thank you," I say, starting my journey back to the surface. The city of Mushrumia is about thirteen miles underground, which is barely deep compared to the large city of Arthropodia. The mining colony caves begin on the surface, and only one cavern leads to Mushrumia, also being the only path that isn't plagued by dangerous gasses.

The miners of the colony have let out so many diseases and dangers that the mine has been shut down for years. Each path, besides one, is taped up and blocked off from public use. The only use people have for it is to get to the Mushrumian kingdom.

I make my way through the caves, past restricted paths, skeletons peeking through the dirt, and random mining tools scattered on the ground. After walking for a few minutes, I get to the makeshift elevator, a single metal platform with a pulley system that the rider needs to operate. The elevator itself is only twelve and a half miles under the surface.

I stand on the highly dangerous platform, grabbing the splintery rope hanging on my left, pulling it down, and feeling the floor below me rise. I must pull myself up twelve and a half miles until I reach the top.

—

After about an hour, I keep one hand on the rope as I check my map. I can see that I've only traveled two miles upwards. The elevator ride down is easy since it just falls at a somewhat slow pace. Everyone dreads the ride-up. As I close my map and continue to pull myself up, the elevator starts to move faster, and so does the rope. Before I know it, I'm being pulled up without me touching the string.

I look up towards the surface, seeing the small hole of light grow more prominent as I approach it. I turn my map on and see the elevation numbers rapidly increase. The elevator shakes a few times as the dirt elevator shaft starts to close. The surface grows closer and closer until I feel the oceanside breeze whisk past my skin.

I finally reach the surface as I stumble from the sudden stop. I look behind me to see the masked man with the sword. He stands broodingly, holding onto the rope with one hand. Behind him are two Garabeshers, their sunken eyes deflecting the sunlight. I stay silent for a moment, waiting to be slaughtered.

"Get off," the man says, pointing his unfinished sword toward Stoean's houses. The crack in his mask that showed his eyes earlier now bleeds darkness. I step off of the platform, keeping my eyes on him.

Does he know I have it? Let's hope not.

I continue to watch him as he steps onto the elevator. The two Garabeshers stay behind, pulling the opposite side of the rope to lower him down. I walk across the sandy beaches of Stoean, walking back into town. The elevator entrance to the mines is barren, with only the wooden pole with the rope through it and the hole down.

There's not even a cover over the elevator—just a hole in the Stoean beaches. The acres of green sand wrap around half of the Stoean, with the rest of the land connecting to other cities.

The beaches are around a few yards from grass to water, and are usually busy. Today, though, the air is brisk and somewhat frozen, and the breeze gives me goosebumps. I feel sand in my boots, so I take them off until I reach the grass.

Stoean is ordered in eighteen rows. The row next to the gates and the one next to the beaches are all stores. The other sixteen rows are houses. Each row is six buildings across. I walk to the closest store to me, which is Austin's Beachside Bar.

The outside of the building is just a rectangle, with a large logo sign on the outside and no color; just a drab light gray and no windows. The doors aren't even glass; they are just pale wood. The bar is held up a few feet with unstable wood planks and has a stone staircase leading to the door.

I make my way up the entry and walk into the candle-lit bar. On my right is the stone bar counter, with a few workers spinning drinks around. Behind them is a bookshelf full of different drinks and glasses. The entire left half of the place is taken up by short, round wooden tables filled with creatures getting drunk.

I spot a few Zargons, some humans, a few masked drinkers, some Arachnavoids, and even a Felishe. Furry humans with small noses, ears on the top of their heads, and eyes with thin pupils. Speaking of Felishes, I see one working behind the counter wearing the bar uniform; black dress pants with a button-down white collared shirt.

This Felishe is different. This one is an old companion of mine. His name is Reez-N, and he's one of the toughest motherfuckers on this planet, and I sort of, somewhat like him. His fur is a dark gray, with hints of a nougat mixed throughout. A few years ago, he used to be a fellow assassin like me, and though he's long past that time, he still has a few scars.

The notable one is a patch of ripped skin above his right eye from a drug deal bust gone wrong near the outskirts of Carishem. It cost the life of another close acquaintance—just another reason I never wanted to step foot into that Gods-forsaken place.

Reez-N's eyes have always stood out to me since they have a profound, blood-like red outline around the pupils, which he's said is a birth defect. So I walk over to the counter and sit on one of the rusted metal stools.

"What brings you back?" Reez-N says without turning his back. Instead, he pours two bottles into one wine glass, which erupts smoke when they touch.

"A Zargon order that?" I jokingly ask.

"As a matter of fact...," he grabs a cup from under the counter full of magma rock, which he pours into the glass. "Yes. How'd you know?"

"Come on, Ree; it's not hard to tell. Their diets equate to volcanic ash." That gets a laugh out of Reez-N, who almost drops the wine glass as he erupts into laughter. So he sets the glass onto the counter, and a black-suited Zargon swipes it.

"He's coming!" someone yells. I turn around to see a blood-covered Arachnavoid run from the doors to the counter.

The front doors burst open, letting in the cold breeze. Everyone grows quiet, with even one or two glass drinks being dropped. I turn my head to see who entered, and none other than the masked man stands with his sword, covered in white blood. I identify it as Mushrumian blood.

He killed them all, trying to find the last piece.

"That guy keeps showing up wherever I go," I say to Reez-N.

He walks into the middle of the room, stabbing his blade into the wooden floor. The doors burst open again, and a woman walks in. She's a foot taller than the man and wears a similar outfit to the man; a black cloak with a white mask. Although, the cloak and mask designs are slightly different. The cape is all black but has white stripes around the sleeves and lacks the metal chest plate.

The mask is a bit longer, with the bottom part extending past the chin. It has two red stripes on either side, extending lower. In the middle is a U-shaped visor, black with a slight red glow around it. While the man's mask has two slits at the mouth area and two tubes from the cheeks, hers has a gray triangular shape over the mouth area and no tubes.

She walks behind the man, and he kneels, keeping one hand on the sword's hilt.

"Good evening, Residents of Loca. We are pleased to be welcomed by your open arms," the woman starts saying, her voice sounding more profound and more robotic than the man.

"And who here has welcomed you? I've seen you on the news. You kill everyone looking for that damn sword piece. Give it a rest; if you haven't found it yet, you never will," a high-voiced patron says from across the room. So I look over at him, and just as I thought, it's a tall, old Orugnic, the same species as Marz.

"Yeah!" the customers explode in unison. The woman slowly turns her head towards the drunkards, and the man tightens his grip on the sword. He stands up and drags the blade across the ground. It cuts up the wooden floor, leaking outside light into the candle-lit room.

He drags the sword around and throws it directly at the Orugnic. It slices clean through the middle of his face, making his face look like a book as it opens up. His body drops onto the table before him, with purple blood splattering on the surrounding drinkers. The sword hits the wall, cracking the stones and making a loud clunk sound.

"As I was saying before being so rudely…interrupted…as we search for the tenth piece of Magona's Sword, crafted by the gods, we shall stay in these abandoned mining colonies. Unfortunately, the past residents…," the woman looks at the Mushrumian blood-covered sword for a moment. "Needed to be evicted from their lives."

"Peace be to Magona," the cloaked man says. He holds up his left arm, with the metal still ripped apart, and a blue glow whisks from the arm cavity. The sword, still in the wall, begins to shake as it shoots from the crack. The blade crumbles down into the hilt, which lands in the man's arm. He folds the corrugated down and attempts to flatten it.

The woman turns around and leaves, and shortly the man follows. I turn to Reez-N, who stands with his hands over his face.

"I thought we got rid of him," he says.

"Hm?" I ask.

"They were here the other day. They were looking for a piece of that sword. Basically ransacked this whole damn town. I guess they're still suspicious or something. Maybe there's a reason they wanted the mining colonies. Poor Mushrumians. Might be extinct now."

"Hopefully, that piece isn't down there," I say, subtly patting the corset over the pocket holding the shard. Then, I give Reez-N a quick smile as I hop off the stool.

"See you around, J!"

"See ya, Ree!" I yell back as I exit through the doors and walk down the stairs. I catch a glimpse of the cloaked duo ascending down into the mines. The breeze begins to pick up as I think to myself.

I need to get rid of this shard. They seem attracted to it…maybe I can destroy it somehow?

My thoughts are interrupted as a buzzing noise vibrates from my hand. I turn my palm towards me and open my map, and a message pops up. KILL HIM YET? I AM WAITING. It's definitely from Marz. I close the popup, recheck my map, and see the marker still pointing in the middle of nowhere.

Time to kill a Mushrumian.

~The Ace~

Being an assassin is a one-person job, but every gun-for-hire knows there's always a backup—or a group of backups. Marz, for example, knows that I'm his best bet but always has someone on standby. Usually, I never know who it is because I get the task done pretty quickly. But since I'm taking too long to even get to Lepio-N's location, I got a message from an old partner of mine.

As I walk along the empty tracks, miles away from Stoean, my hand buzzes. I slow my pace and open up my map. Two popups show, and I read them slowly. WHAT IS TAKING YOU SO LONG? I roll my eyes and close the first message. I could tell it was from Marz just by the entirely capital message. The second popup enlarges, and I read it. Hey JX, wanna race to Lepio? You got a head start, yet I'm closer than you are to him. MZ is losing his faith in youuuuu -M-A.

This asshole.

Seven years ago, I was partnered with a Canilupus, a breed similar to Felishes but with protruding, snout-like noses, taller ears, and sharp fangs. This Canilupus's name is Ace, but his code name is Metal. Hence the M-A abbreviation; it stands for Metal Ace. The mission we were on was a double job.

I had someone I had to kill; he had someone else. We were only together because our targets were at a party down in Leath. Ever since that mission, he's been obsessed. He's wanted to be the best assassin on Loca, but there's a reason he's not.

I do it as quickly as I can. Ace, however, enjoys killing in the most gruesome, slow ways possible. One of my big reasons I can't let him kill Lepio-N. Another one? Cloning is a concept Locanagwan scientists have dabbled in but never fully understood. Certain species have been brought back from extinction, and I believe that if I get some Mushrumian DNA, I could donate it. So if Ace gets to Lepio-N before me, he'll splatter that DNA all over the walls.

The sound of a train horn snaps me out of my thoughtful trance. I turn to see the oncoming train and swiftly jump back onto the grass. Then, as the train passes me, it slows down. Confused, I turn to see where it's headed. Then, I focus on a large building, the Leathean Train Station.

How'd I get here that fast? How long was I thinking for?

I realize the grass I'm standing on is a dark blue, and the black trees around me twist around themselves. I walk up to the train station, which is identical to the Lükahmp station. I pass through the hordes of rushing creatures into the thin city of Leath.

Leath is the twice-removed cousin of the Locanagwan cities. Being the second to last city built before I was born, Leath is a city that's one long strip, about two miles across and fifty-five miles long. Like I said, just a strip of a town. The houses are nothing special, just standard stone huts like in Carishem. Although, unlike that walled-in shitshow, Leath's cabins are cleaned daily and aren't covered in moist moss.

Leath has a road system connecting all houses and stores, but nobody uses them. They're more for show so that people think this city has some worth. Leath has as much worth as Carishem's mayor.

I step out of the concerningly busy station onto the damp pavement roads. I look to the gray clouds, sensing another rain storm. It seems like it rains every other day here, and it's ironic since one of our moons, Yogan, is made of molten rock. Unlike Stoean's organized houses, Leath just has buildings scattered like a dumped-out puzzle set.

Across the street, I see a fully transparent restaurant named Austin's Watching You Eat! The walls, ceiling, and floor of the two-floor building are all glass. Patrons sit on glass chairs at glass tables. All of the local Locanagwan food is delivered in mirror boxes.

"Hello, JX. Seems like a while since our little Stoean house raid...we ended on such bad terms. Parting ways as a little kid watched us walk away with the head of his sister?," a deep, somewhat seductive voice calls behind me. A voice that makes me squint my eyes in annoyance. I put on an obviously fake smile and slowly turn around to see a tall, extremely tall Ace. His appearance has changed since I last saw him several years ago.

He has dyed light gray fur, crimson eyes, and a baby blue nose on the tip of his slightly crooked snout. On the top of his head is a light green fluff of hair, which sits between his ears and covers his right eye. Speaking of eyes, his left one has a deep scar over it.

As for clothes, he sports a yellow cloth poncho, a weathered purple leather tunic, some soaked black rain pants, and boots muddier than two Piggians wrestling after a storm. His hands are covered with purple leather gloves, blending into the top's sleeves.

"Funny thing, Ace, I was just thinking about you. I saw your message a few minutes ago. You've been waiting for me, I see," I sarcastically say to him. He lets out a deep laugh, which bounces his fluff of hair.

"How cute. You DOOOOO still think about meee," he says in a high-pitched voice. He holds his hands over his cheeks and gives me puppy dog eyes. So I try to keep the fake smile together.

"Yep. Such a COMMON occurrence," I say through ever clenching teeth. My cheeks begin to shake as I continue to strain my facial muscles. I can feel my left eye twitch as Ace looks at me with a smug half-smile. He whisks away, walking into the restaurant. I stand for another few moments with my fake smile, which now looks like I'm being forced to show my teeth.

That got rid of him. I should be able to get ahead of him now that he's taking a break.

I quickly open my map, holding my arm against my chest to keep it hidden. It opens, slightly hurting my eyes as the blue glow of the hologram shines in them. I check for the marker's location; just like I imagined, it's still in the middle of nowhere. Compared to my location, it's only a few miles away. So I have to walk off the Leath strip into the wilderness to get to Lepio-N.

"What's that, young miss?" I hear from behind me. I slowly turn around to see some elderly Pēchauck, hunched over with a walking cane made of Felishe bones. Pēchaucks are elegant creatures; stubby flyers with long necks, small heads, and very skinny arms. Their legs are extremely slender, with four small toe-like bones poking out. Their bodies are just circles decorated with colorful hairs.

They have large feathers that extrude from their back, acting as a symbol of their wisdom. They have eyes on the sides of their faces, which means they move their head from side to side while talking or looking at people. All Pēchaucks are colorful, as stated earlier, and this one is no different. The color on this one is strawberry blonde, with a mix of teal throughout. Highlights of gray appear at the head of the Pēchauck due to its age.

"Excuse me?" I ask. The Pēchauck moves its head wildly to look at me, getting closer each time.

"What is that? Are you a SPY or something?"

I stare at the Pēchauck with a confused expression, wondering who they thought they were.

"What's your name?" I slowly ask, backing up every time it gets closer. The Pēchauck stops moving and positions its neck up while looking down at me.

"It is Mayor Hail Lēy of Leath, and you have contraband. Holographic maps are BANNED in this city," she booms with anger. What feels like gallons of spit splash across my face as I smell her minty breath. Then, after she closes her vast mouth, I open my eyes and stare at her for a few moments. A brisk wind blasts through, blowing my hair and Hail's many feathers around.

"I'll just be on my w-," I start to say as I slowly begin to walk away.

"DON'T PULL IT OUT AGAIN!" she yells sternly. I pause after she shouts at me before I run away from the inflamed Pēchauck. My boots slam against the concrete roads as I run into the city, away from any authorities.

—

After a while of running, I decide to take a break and sit down at one of the restaurants. I've passed by a few; some looked like beautifully crafted buildings, and others looked like medical stores. This one seems like a drug house, with boarded-up windows, three stories, and a complete brick exterior. The double glass entrance doors are covered in poorly nailed planks.

I look at the neon pink sign above the front doors that reads: Austin's Zargles. What's a Zargle? The only good thing that came from Zargonic cultures. It's a mixture of Leathean Belgagor berries and the meat from wild Schtarpfiches. Schtarpfiches are five to six-foot tall creatures with six arms that protrude in each direction. Its body is flat and scaly and is only there to connect the arms. They have no eyes, mouth, nose, or ears. They just lie on the ground, birthing baby Schtarpfiches every five weeks.

Before I step into the Zargle eatery, I look around the street. On my left and right are endless rows of buildings built out of everyday materials. They vary in size, anywhere from one to seven stories tall. The clean concrete roads remain unscathed, and the sun paints yellow streaks through the dark blue sky.

It's about seven at night.

I snap myself out of my hesitation and push open the creaky doors. The inside lights blind me for a moment. I blink my eyes a few times and look around at the disheveled restaurant. On the outside, it looked like a medium-sized building, but it feels much more claustrophobic inside. The room hits me with the smell of rot and mold.

Rows of cushiony blue booths are now nothing but the metal frame. The tables are all cracked and broken. Dirty plates, crumbs, and chunks of food lie in every corner and crevice of the walls. The back counter is made up of smashed glass and occupied by a few apron-wearing Zargons.

Next to the counter is a pool table with dirty, cracked balls and three Zargons wearing spiked black jackets, high black boots, and no pants. It shows off their scaly legs, covered in blood and grease. They are part of the Dismayed Waltzers group, a clan that works under the reign of Lord Garzan and live on the opposite side of Loca from here, in a large stone castle named Castle Pobomba.

I sit in one of the booths that still have some cushions left. Across the table sits a shady man hunched over a white plate of purple Belgagor berries. He wears the same kind of cloak as the man with the sword. Gray robes and a black leather belt over the waist. His hands are bloodied and scratched, with bruises and dirt caked around the bony knuckles. His face is covered with his hood, and I can only see a dark, skinny nose.

"I hope you don't mind if I sit here. None of the other tables looked…together," I say as I sit down. I stare at him awkwardly, not sure if he is even awake. Or alive.

"Order." A brooding voice jolts me out of my staring as I turn to see a female Zargon. A dark, grassy green one with two broken horns and poorly applied red lipstick. She holds a small stone and a dismembered, blood-covered finger in one hand.

"What's the menu?" I slowly ask. The Zargon squints her eyes. I lean back slightly in fear.

"Today's specials are the Zargle Deluxe, the Zargle Pargle, and the Gorshaken bowl," she says in a one-note voice.

Gorshaken sounds nice.

"I'll have the Gorshaken bowl," I decide. A Gorshaken bowl is a mixture of exotic meat from the Kingdom of Dommis Triang, on the other side of Loca. The Zargon splashes the finger across the stone and walks away. I fold my hands together and place them on the table as I see the man move.

He looks up at me, and I get a good look at his face. Dark skin and a bony, malnourished shape. Droopy eyelids that cover his neon green eyes. A mouth that doesn't move up or down, a perfect poker face. His cheeks are so sunken in that they're probably only a millimeter thick. He holds his arms up and lowers his hood, showing off his straight, long, snow-white hair that trickles down to his shoulders.

"Janx?" he says in a low, monotone voice. His voice sounds like it's coming from behind me.

"You know me?" I ask, my voice being higher than usual. The man moves his head toward me and squints his eyes. He points to the left side of my chest.

"It's in there? How are you still alive?" he asks, with a higher pitch. I look down my corset to see the glowing shard illuminating my scratched, bare stomach. The man jumps onto the table, shoving his hand down my top, scraping my left boob. Before I can grab his arm, he latches his bony fingers onto the shard and yanks it out.

On the way out, the shard cuts the middle of my chest, and I quickly grab a tissue from my pockets. I shove it into my upper chest and hold it with my right hand as I pull a knife out with my left. I like my small pocket knife the most, with a black handle wrapped with rope and a freshly cleaned gold blade.

I hold it to his throat as he holds the shard above his head. He shines with the bit of light coming from the boarded windows behind me. The orange shine glows across his face and turns his hair a light orange.

"This is real. How are you still alive?" he asks, turning only his eyes to me, not his head. I open my mouth to speak when a crash sends a shock wave into my back. "We'll continue this later; meet me under the Bleeding Tree."

I turn around to see what made the noise, not noticing the man jump out of view. A large shape stands on the crushed doors, illuminating only the back. He steps into the light, which reveals Al-X himself.

A fat, sunburnt, white, round face with prominent cheeks and thick eyebrows that hover over small, squinted eyes. A pair of thinly framed glasses sink into his plump nose. A thick goatee loosely sticks to his chin of rolls. A messy black mullet perches atop his dry forehead, covered in flakes of skin and dandruff. Shining light reflects off his black suit, with sleeves that show off his hairy arms. Around his waist is a brown leather belt, with a golden handgun peeking itself out from a holster on the side.

His large body and heavy weight shatter the glass as he steps across the doors into the building. He looks around at the patrons, using his tall body to strike fear into them. In the background, I can hear a plate crash onto the hard floor. One of the waiters runs out from the kitchen and drops to his knees in front of Al-X.

"Al-X, what brings you here?" it asks, bowing its head onto the soiled tiles that line the eating area. I can see tears dropping onto the ground. Al-X readjusts the collar on his suit and pulls out his handgun, a small, one-barrel pistol with etching on the sides that I cannot make out from my distance.

He pulls a clip out from the inside of his suit and loads it into the bottom of the handle. He cocks it back, then pulls the trigger. A bullet blasts into the bowing Zargon's head, spraying brain and blood mixed with the dirt and tears. Everyone in the room screams as Al-X lifts his head; his expression is that of a bloodthirsty psychopath.

"One." His voice deepens through the world, somehow saying it in two syllables.

He aims his pistol at a group of Zargons on the other side of the room, and each one lifts their arms above their head. A large smile cracks through the dry cheeks on Al-X's face as his moldy yellow teeth shine in the light.

"Seen a female Arachnavoid anywhere?" he asks. His grimy fangs grind against each other as the Zargons all shake their heads in confusion. "No? Such a shame…."

The next moment, each Zargon is shot in the head, blood splashes onto the oily walls, and each body slams onto the ground, cracking the fragile tiles.

"Two…three…four…five…," Al-X counts with each casing tapping the ceramic floor. Each tap makes a very quiet dink masked with each trigger pull. Three Zargons burst from the heavy kitchen doors, running past me, holding metal knives.

"You clinker!" one of them yells. Al-X, without turning his head from the left side of the building, shoots each one through their tough, scaly foreheads. Each body limply splats onto the ground, with some blood flying onto the toes of my shiny black boots.

"Six…seven…eight," he counts again. Finally, he points toward me. His smile edges to the left of his crusty visage. His finger slides off of the trigger, retreating to the grip. "You're lucky there were nine in this building. I would've bursted your balls faster than a Probos in a minefield."

His hand drops to his side and returns the gun to his suit pocket. He lets out a harsh, cracking laugh which makes me flinch. I slide my hand behind me, touching around to find the shape of my gun. Before I can locate it, Al-X sighs and his eyes notice my arm movements.

"I never asked you. Have you seen an Arachnavoid running and trying to hide?" his laughing lips fade to sovereignty. I bring my arm to a halt.

"I think she went that way," I say, stupidly pointing in the direction of my marker. Al-X nods his head and flashes a quick smile. He turns around, his feet shattering the glass and wood beneath them. Once he is out of view, I relax my whole body, exhaling hard.

I turn to talk to the mysterious man, but he is no longer there. I look over at the Zargon corpses, feeling slightly remorseful but glad they're dead. I feel the familiar vibration of a message, so I slide my shaking fingers down my arm to open my map. The usual popup appears, telling me I'm too late.

M-A GOT THE REWARD. THREW IN A LITTLE EXTRA. WHAT IS WRONG WITH YOU?

"J? What the hell happened in here? I was coming down to get some food for my friends," I hear from my left. I quickly close my fist to hide the map as I swiftly turn my head. A Felishe stands on the crushed doors, avoiding the shards of glass that stick up. The fur on his body is dark gray, and streaks of nougat shine through. An emerald shining green kirtle stretches down to the black spiked clogs on his soft body.

"Reez?" I cry out. "You don't even want to know."

"Are you hurt? There are damn ZARGON corpses over there. Did you do that?" Reez laughs.

"Am I hurt? Reez, are YOU hurt? What kind of outfit is that? And no, I did not kill them; Al-X did." After hearing my words, Reez's smile and laughter fade. He looks toward the ground as his composure sinks. I quickly take note. "So, where are you off to?"

Reez ignores my question.

"Why was he here?" he asks, his voice now cold and grim. His eyes fixate on mine. "I'm sorry, I have to go. I can't tell you now, but I'll send some allies to pick you up. Stay here"

He quickly runs out of the building and into the distance, and I slam my fist on the table. The wooden tabletop cracks under my force.

"WHY AM I BEING LEFT IN THE DARK RIGHT NOW?" I yell out in angst to the body-ridden, empty restaurant. My yells are only met with the buzzing of the electric lights and occasional chirp from outside. I plop back onto the broken seat, which tilts backward. I drop my head onto the wall on my right. From the fingerprint-ridden windows on the kitchen doors, I can see the shape of a face. I tilt my head straight, trying to identify them.

"Come out already; I've had it with the number of people appearing in this place," I groan. I wait for a response but do not receive one. I bite my lips as I grow impatient from the watcher's lack of movement. My eyes roll on their own as I scoot myself from the seat, hearing a few bones crack as I stand up. "Can you just come out already?"

From the window, I can see the watcher shake his head. I rub my forehead, thinking it's just some prop on the other side. I reach the double kitchen doors, and as I open them, an arm bursts between them, grabbing my right thigh. The arm is dark and covered in black goo, pulsating in strips along the skin. It pulls on my leg, tugging my leg forward. The back of my head nosedives onto the floor as I'm drawn through the doors into the kitchen.

I'm dragged through the maze-like cooking area, past tables covered in dirty silverware, misplaced dishwashers, dirty bags of fish, and other unsanitary oddities. The whole place has a dirty, grunge smell, and grime is caked on every surface possible. The arm continues to heave me through as I wonder how long the arm is. I pull my flailing arms down to grab a weapon, but scattered pots and pans knock into them.

Finally, the arm hauls me into the backroom, guarded by loose, blood-soaked vinyl strip curtains. It drops my leg right in front of the doorway, disappearing into the room. I slowly sit up as the arm appears from the curtains, ushering me in.

I kick myself onto my feet, hearing a crack or two from my legs. I walk through the curtains, pushing them aside, into a small, empty room. In the middle, however, is a short wooden stool. Sitting on top of it is the man from before. Neon green eyes, dark skin, long white hair. He holds the glowing orange shard up with his left thumb and pointer.

"You? I thought you left me for dead," I yell out. His face remains unchanged, a flat smile with unblinking eyes. He puts his middle finger on the shard. "Hello? Are you going to say anything?"

He puts his ring finger up. I stare at him in anger. He slowly raises his pinky, and his entire body jumps when it touches the shard. The black goo from before begins to seep out of his skin, almost phasing through it. It continues to pulse, slithering across his body until he removes a finger from the shard. The goo retracts, making a sloppy sound.

"This shard has destructive properties. I still don't understand how you were able to keep it with you," he finally spits out. His voice continues to bounce around the room. He throws the shard into the air, and it falls right onto his lap.

"What do you mean, dangerous properties?" I ask. His flat mouth raises on the right. He grabs the shard with two fingers and throws it at me. I catch it in my arms.

"Grab that with your hand. Doesn't matter which one," he says. He points at the shard. I look down, letting it roll down my arm into my right hand. I grasp it in my hand, secretly not letting my pinky touch it. "See? Nothing happens when you have it."

"Pity," I sarcastically say. I throw the shard back at him, which he catches with three fingers. "Look, I gotta get on my way. I need to go back to my apartment."

I begin to walk away as the man grabs onto my arm. Then, I turn around, pulling my arm out of his grip. Finally, he raises a finger at me.

"What city do you live in? Lükahmp?" he asks with graveness. His eyes widen as he says it. I look down at him, hiding my fear.

"Why? What's it to you?" I say after swallowing air. He finally blinks after hearing me.

"I overheard Al-X telling one of his minions to search the Lükahmp hotels tonight. He's searching for one of his runaway wives."

"When? When did you hear that? Tell me!" I yell, hovering over the man, his eyelids bow down.

"After he left the building, I was hiding out there. He came and left in a rush. One of his dice bots is on their way there now." Before he can finish, I turn away and run.

I bolt out of the kitchen through the vinyl curtains, double doors, and the broken front entrance. I set my sights on the train station, hoping I can make it on the next ride. My boots slap against the harsh pavement as people watch from the sidewalks. I can feel their looks of judgment as I rush through the road, but their faces are blanked out in my mind.

My thighs begin to numb.

The train station gets closer and closer as I approach it, seems like it's the one moving. From the corner of my eye, I can see the glass restaurant from before, peeking out from behind other buildings. I can see Ace staring at me, smiling as I pass it. His fur and clothes are dotted with dried splashes of blood. He holds a dirty cross-shaped item in his hand, with one of the ends sharpened, most likely by his teeth.

My calves begin to numb.

I turn my attention away from Ace, setting my sights back on the station. I'm closer now, about ten yards away. I reach the stairs leading up, awkwardly skipping every other step.

My chest begins to numb.

I run through the front glass doors, shattering them and cutting my arms in the process. Some shards remain lodged in my skin, but I pay no attention to them. All the trains are gone, except one that goes straight to Lükahmp. All the doors slowly begin to close, so I sprint faster. I bolt across the wooden train station floor, passing rows of seating filled with creatures, all watching me.

My arms begin to numb.

Before the doors fully close, I dive in between them. The metallic doors fully shut as soon as my entire body passes them. I quickly stand myself up, brushing the dirt from the ground off of my clothes. Only a few passengers are in this car, and they're all either sleeping or too tired to pay attention to my entrance.

My whole body feels numb.

I sit on one of the chipped green leather booths, right next to a Horae. Horaes are sentient creatures, usually a soul bound to an inanimate object. This one has the appearance of an Earth grandfather clock, with a large clock face over the top of a glass cabinet with a pendulum forever swinging inside. The wood around the front is made of clean redwood, with two arches on the top coming together to form a tall, skinny beam.

At the bottom of his grandfather's clock body, a wooden skirt covers red, green, and black plaid pants. They are rolled up, showing off some expensive white boots. Sprouting from his sides are two arms, ending with round jointed fingers. Hundreds of watches, all sizes and showing different times, are along the arms and legs.

My eyelids droop as I doze off, and images of dancing grandfather clock Horaes fill my head as I wait.

———

The train comes to a screeching halt, knocking me out of my sleep. I look out the window to see my apartment building, seemingly untouched. I wait for the doors to open, and I rush out, knocking over some randos in my way. I run through the station to my apartment building.

I run to the apartment door, slowly turning the knob as I regain my feeling. I push the door open, leaning forward against it. When the door comes to a stop, I stumble along onto the floor. My jaw cracks as it slams onto the hard, cold floor. I stay on the ground, sighing as the pain grows. I use my foot to close the door from the floor.

"Are you ok?" I hear from above me. I roll onto my back to see Arachcait leaning over my head. I turn my head slightly to the side as I realize who it is.

"You're still here!" I yell. She doesn't respond, so I open my mouth to continue, but she cuts me off.

"Did you get some food?"

Food? Did I promise her food?

"I didn't get food, sorry," I say calmly. "Listen. Is Al-X the big man that's chasing you?"

Arachcait looks shocked and doesn't immediately respond. Her eyelids droop down, and she begins to bite her fingers. I stand up, walking over to my worn couch. I sit down and start to whisper to her.

"We need to get out of here. Al-X will search this place; you can't be here when he does." I begin to space out as I think about where to go.

The sound of knocking snaps me back into reality. I suddenly sit up, facing the door, which provides another knock. Then, I push myself up with my hands and trip over to the door. Then, as I place my hand onto the cold, greasy doorknob, Arachcait rests her hand on my shoulder and whispers into my ear.

"I'm going to your room in case it's him."

I open the door, and two characters appear from the hallway. A woman made of multicolored green grass and leaves stands before me. Gray smoke flows from little holes in her body. Her eyes have deep red clouds around the dark green pupils. Through small cavities throughout her body, I can see inside.

She has a skeleton-like frame made of thin sticks and, oddly, a small fire in the stomach region. The flames never grow or shrink, and the smoke rises above it. Behind her is a large Varmpur, a forest predator, just a human with sharp teeth and a thirst for blood.

This Varmpur has a big build, dark skin, no hair, and a smile that shows his sharp incisors. He wears dark gray robes and has a sheath with a serrated sword.

"Hello. We are your new next-door roommates! My name is Juwles, and this is my childhood friend, Juwle-N. We just wanted to say our greetings, and we'll be out of your hair now!" the plant woman says, her mouth shaking the leaves around her face. I stand confused, not responding. After a few seconds of awkward silence, Juwles' smile is covered by leaves as she looks around the hallway.

She steps toward me, positioning herself as into the room as she can. She signals to Juwle-N with her right hand and closes the door with her left. I try to open the door, but Juwles grabs onto my arm. Her touch feels very soft and slightly moist.

"Listen. You're in danger. Al-X has some minions on the first floor right now. Anyone who doesn't let them search their room is being killed. They're looking for a girl, but they're also looking for people in the Nuvorwurld

Revolution," Juwles says quickly. I stutter out words, trying to respond to that.

"Good, that group is bad. I've heard about it from my boss; they're full of evil people," I finally stammer. Juwles starts to plead with me, trying to stop me from talking.

"What are you talking about? How could you say this when you're friends with the leader?" she yells out. I step back into the kitchen, trying to grab onto the counter for support.

"What do you mean?" I scream back at her. "Who are you?"

"Reez! Reez is the leader of our group. He sent us here to check on you, to make sure you are safe," she explains. She tries to calm me down by rubbing my arm, but I slap it away. "We use the N surname to identify ourselves."

"No. No, no, no, no. You're lying," I spurt out, interrupting Juwles. I look into her red eyes, trying to tell if she's lying. Her eyes remain stationed on me, a clear sign that she is telling the truth. My arm gives way, and I hit the counter. It crashes into my side, which I don't even feel as I sense the room start to spin.

I fall onto the ground, slamming into one of the open cabinets. Juwles tries to hold me up, but her stick arms fold under my pressure. I can see Juwles call out to her partner, but my ears drain all audio in exchange for an ever-increasing loud ringing noise. Everything begins to duplicate as my vision dwindles.

—

My vision and feelings are restored as I feel water being poured into my mouth. I blink my eyes back to normal to see Juwles holding a glass of water above me.

"You're back? Good, we have to get out NOW," she yells to me. Knocking comes from the door, and Juwle-N runs over and blocks it with his large build. Juwles grabs my arm and pulls me up, and I stumble to catch my balance. Then, I rip my arm from her grasp.

"I'm not coming with you traitors," I argue. Juwles turns around, and the flame inside her grows, as does the smell radiating off her. She tries to speak as the knocking gets louder.

"Will you check that?" Juwles yells to Juwle-N. He rolls his eyes as he puts his hand onto the knob. "Anyways, just listen. Whatever you know about the revolution is wrong. Just come wi-."

An explosion from the door launches Juwle-N through the glass doors across the room. Juwles is thrown over me, into the kitchen wall. The blast kicks me over the kitchen counter, falling onto the ash-ridden couch. Once the eruption ends, the outside hallway is filled with the screams of victims and the ceiling crashing.

I roll myself off the couch toward the broken glass window. All the sharp, broken shards around the hole are draped in the pale white blood of Juwle-N. Ash and dirt cover all open surfaces, as well as my body. I look up at the ceiling, which is now catching fire.

I reach into my corset to pull out one of my medicare needles and think I pull one out. It's a small capsule full of some sort of liquid. I open it with my shaking arms, but the top shoots off, hitting me in the left eye. My hands move in front of my eyes, and I accidentally spill the liquid over the right side of my face.

The bitter smell hits me immediately, and I realize it's not my medicare. I rub my left eye as the liquid begins to stream down my body. So I grab one of the dirty cushions and try to wipe it off, but that only spreads it out more.

I roll over onto my stomach to see if there's anything else I can use as a large chunk of the ceiling lands on my back. It cracks my spine, and I feel a sharp pain around it. I turn onto my back again, looking down at my stomach. The chunk of ceiling falls onto the ground as a small patch of fire spreads onto my right arm.

The liquid smeared all over my body begins to ignite, feeling like a million knives are being stabbed into the right side of my person. I start screaming as the fire distorts my skin into molds of flesh. Thin patches of skin are melded over my right eye and my ear. The hair begins to burn to a crisp, and my corset is mixing with my stomach and chest. The right half of my leggings are burned straight to the bone. The complete left side of my body is left intact as the rest continues to go up in flames.

My voice tries to scream more, but it only warps and bends as the flames overtake it. Another crash is heard from above, and a gust of wind wipes through the room.

The breeze calms down the inferno atop my body, but just as I begin to think it's over, the rest of the ceiling collapses atop me.

~The Arthropodians~

I hate being underground. I'm not claustrophobic, I just hate the idea of being trapped underground, and nobody can find you. So while I've never been in Arthropodia, I've known about it for years. It IS the largest city in Loca, after all. Although, it's underground, so it technically doesn't count.

My burned body pulls itself out from under some heavy rocks into some light. I find myself in the destroyed apartment waiting room. Stones and debris cover what used to be an empty room full of only chairs. Across from me is the doorway out, which leads into darkness. I crack my left pointer finger, barely being able to move my numb right arm. The nail lights up, and the room is lit up.

I slowly walk out of the disheveled waiting room into a large cave. The air instantly becomes cold. Solidified brown dirt builds up the uneven walls, leading further into the planet's depths. Webs are frequent, covering large patches of the wall decorated with dismembered, dried-up body parts. My boots make a squishy sound against the slightly soft ground.

"How long is this going to take?" My voice now sounds very scratchy and deformed.

—

After what feels like hours of walking, I finally come across a landmark. A wooden door is oddly placed on the floor at a random point in this cavern. It's a chipped brown with a golden doorknob. I stop before it, thinking how much of a trap it is. So I step over it and continue through the depths.

—

After an even more extended amount of walking, I see a light at the end of the cavern. A natural light, one that looks yellow and paints the walls a lighter brown. The spider webs have grown plenty, as well. The cavern opens broader and taller as I approach the light until the exit is large enough to fit a stone hut. The light basks over me, and I feel my skin warm up. Once the light fades into the background, I am met by a large city. Dirt houses and buildings reach up high, almost to the surface of Loca. It seems like I am miles underground, and this city is closer to the core than the top.

I open my map, and my location shows that I'm almost three hundred miles under. I can see hundreds, if not thousands, of Arachnavoids walking around. Six armed creatures with different hairstyles, colors, and heights. I can see some crawl up the sides of buildings, some crawl on all eights while carrying boxes on their back, and some even walk on just their legs. A large tube in the middle of the city reaches up all the way through the surface, letting a small ounce of natural sunlight shine through.

The surface of the city's cavern walls is the same as the rest but covered in protective webbing all throughout. I stand in awe at the town of Arachnavoids as I notice one stumbling towards me. An old one, with a hunched back and long gray hair. His eyes are all squinting, and he sports a webbed-together dirt crown.

"Hello. I am King Whittene of Arthropodia," he says in an old, shattered voice. "You must be one of the survivors of the collapse. Come, others are waiting."

He directs me to follow him through the streets. Along the way, I make small conversation with him.

"Do you know what caused that explosion? Did you have anything to do with it?" I ask with sincerity.

"No, we are afraid we do not know," he responds. "Although, all bets are on Al-X since he has direct access from his casino to the Arthropodian mines."

"Why does everyone point to Al-X being behind everything? I know he's out for everyone's money, but there's a whole revolution trying to kill him for no reason. He's just a corrupt manager."

Whittene stops and looks at me for a moment, all eight eyes staring into me.

"No reason?" he aggressively asks. "Who told you that?"

"A close friend. Someone I work for," I say. He shakes his head and continues walking. "What? Why is everyone on the side of the revolution?"

"Whomever your 'friend' may be, they are certainly with Al-X," Whittene snaps at me. I grow agitated at this old Arthropodian. "Just go into that building with the rest."

He points at a three-story dirt building, held together by webbing and dried mud. A sign made of sticks on the front reads Arthropodia Medical Home. I walk through the open entrance, seeing rows of beds with the apartment victims lying on them. Most are asleep or dead, but some are talking to the Arthropodian medical staff.

Among the living, I can see Juwles, who lacks her left leg. A tangle of plants and leaves wrapped around a jagged twig remain where her thigh formerly connected. A small clear tube protrudes from her right arm. It's connected to a bag of some off-white liquid hanging from a pole suspended in the air with webs. Lying among the dead, however, I spot Juwle-N. His pale skin is hidden by the mix of dirt and yellow Varmpur blood covering it.

I step over the bodies of different tenants; some that I know and some that I don't. Some with only a tiny wound, some only a head. I reach the table with Juwles on it, and she steadily opens her cloudy eyes. Her breathing is heavy.

"Janx," she says, taking her time with each syllable. "They dug us out from the rubble. They sent some more searchers to get more, but you must have slipped by them."

"Where is Reez?" I ask. She breaks eye contact.

"Janx, please, it is not a good ti-."

"Where is he?"

Juwles sighs and looks back at me. I can feel my face grow red. She continues to hesitate until I grab onto her viny throat. I crunch some leaves under my grip. She doesn't choke, but the fire inside her flickers. I raise my other hand up in a fist.

"Where is Reez? I need to talk to him. Now."

"He's busy right now," Juwles says, her voice grasping for freedom. My eyebrows dropdown. I pull her off the table from her throat, slamming her face to the ground. Some of the staff turn their heads toward me.

"Mind your business," I yell at them. I turn my attention to Juwles, swiping fallen leaves into her stomach. Then, I grab onto some leaves on the back of her head, pulling back and listening as the neck creaks.

"Janx, please, calm yourself down," Juwles pleads. I ignore her and slam her face into the solid dirt ground. I let go, cursing as I look around at all of the eyes. I slowly stand up and walk back into the Arthropodian streets, passing by mistrustful organisms. Then, as I walk through the Medical Home doors, I can hear the rustling of Athropodians struggling to lift Juwles back onto her bed.

I step onto the squishy dirt paths, roaming around, passing by dirt and web-made structures, which are home to many Arthropodians. I backtrack to the cave where I came from. I look through the darkness, noticing a new opening in the cavern walls. I slowly put one foot in front of the other, creeping toward it. Then, as I get closer, a pair of tiny orange lights blink from the cavity of shadows.

I pause my pace as the double lights seem to move toward me. I swivel around, prepared to retreat back to the Medical Home. One foot hits the dirt in front of me as something grabs onto the edge of my corset. It pulls back, cracking my spine as my body flings backward. I hit the ground, my hair landing in a puddle of greasy brown mud.

I begin muttering to myself as I raise my head out of the pool of sludge.

The brown liquid drips from my head as the two orange eyes grow from the darkness. Following them into the light is a salmon face, with large frowning lips that stretch from both cheeks. Black eyebrows almost cover the cavities where the eyes should be. Flames ripple from his scorched head, flowing in the soft air. I look down at his wear, a bright orange jumpsuit that matches his flaming appearance. The bottom of the pant legs are burned almost to the knees, and smoke rises from underneath his bare feet.

A tear in the fabric near his neck reveals a hole through his chest. Dangling from a few tangled veins, his heart beats violently, surrounded by cracked black ribs. Lava-filled capillaries stretch out from the skin around his beating core. They flow through his body, visible on his legs, arms, and the base of his neck. He holds both arms above me, and chains around his wrists rattle as they sway around.

"Where am I?" he asks. His voice sounds cracked and deep, just like popping lava. "I don't know how I got here."

"Who are you?" I ask, pushing myself up. "And why did you pull me like that? My back pains are going to be worse now."

"I apologize; I am getting used to the energetic pull. My name is…I can't remember. My brain is still fuzzy, but things ARE coming back to me…." He rubs his head, and ash falls off like dandruff. "Can you take me to someone? A medical station or…or…just anyone?"

"I just came from somewhere that can treat you. Come on," I say, leading him toward the Medical Home. Along the walk, the Arthropodians cower in fear in their webbed dirt houses, watching the fire man as he leaves burnt footprints on the soft ground. The environment is now like a ghost town compared to when I left the Medical Home. So we turn down a street corner where the building is, being greeted by Juwles, whose grassy body radiates an odd smell.

"Janx, please, at least just hear us out," she tries to say. I point my finger into her face, pressing against her leafy face.

"Listen to me, you smelly lawn decoration; I need to speak to Reez directly," I yell at her. "I really don't trust you."

Juwles looks at me, too stunned to speak, holding her forehead with her hands.

"Janx, just get out of here."

I stare back at her; we both remain unblinking. She turns around, heading back into the medical building. I hear voices of Arthropodians calming her down and helping her to her bed. I turn around to face the fire man staring into space.

"Hey, blaze boy, I don't think I can follow you in there," I point to the medical place. "But you should get some care there."

"Blaze boy...blaze...I like that name...basic, but to the point," he says, ignoring everything else I said. His eyes still stare into nothing as he nods, thinking about the name. So I snap my fingers in front of his face, which brings him to.

"Yo, get in there. Get your memory back before you forget more," I say. I put my hands on his shoulders, pushing him toward the building. He reluctantly walks through the doors, out of my sight.

"Excuse me, miss," a frail voice asks from my left. I turn to see an old hunched-over Arthropodian with gray hair tied in a bun crawling on a wooden cane. Her six arms carry her two limp legs along the ground. "You should be careful around those Infrens, especially with those scars. Dangerous creatures, they are. Walking around with their hotheads."

"He's an Infren? I thought they went extinct during some flood a few years back," I ask, examining my shriveled and burnt right arm. The old lady holds onto the cane with all six arms, pulling herself up and using it as stability. We both turn to face the medical building.

"That's what the people say, although I beg to differ. With all those wildfires happening in the Southern Stegion area, I think they're hiding away. Anyways, sorry for the lecture. Just thought you should know."

"Should I get him out?" I turn to the old Arthropodian, who has disappeared. I shrug it off. I walk through the streets, seeing them become more populated as the frightened Arthropodians come out from their hiding. I see the long tube that reaches the surface past the high dirt towers and webbed ziplines. I believe an elevator there will lift me back to safety. Buzzing on my arm makes me jump. I swipe it, and my map opens up. A notification reading IF YOU DO NOT GET BACK TO ME BEFORE SUNSET, YOU ARE DONE.

Knowing Marz, me being 'done' doesn't just mean fired.

I reach the clear tube and, sure enough, at the bottom is a small chamber of buttons. I step in, and it shoots upward before I can turn around. I look at the bleeding orange sky through the elevator's window roof. I look down at the city of Arthropodia, which shrinks as I rise. The elevator's speed is identical to the platform to the Mushrumian caves. The platform stops at the surface, leading to a small makeshift shed. It's a pile of rusted brown sheets of metal held together with Arachnavoid webbing.

I push on some of the sheets, which knocks over all of them, and they clang on the soft Lükahmp grass. I find myself on the outskirts, conveniently right behind the nightclub. In the air, I can see the smoke from the apartment destruction miles in the distance. I look behind to see the usual, distorting trees surrounding the club's back. As I pass the warping, curved trees, something catches my eye. A symbol is carved into one of the tree trunks: a half circle underneath two X shapes with a circle behind it all. I walk up to the tree, placing my hand on the trunk. Red, blood-like liquid seeps from the wood. It's a bleeding tree. The bark gives way, and I fall into the tree.

I bounce down a dirt slide into a small, dark concrete entranceway. I pull myself onto my feet, seeing a welded-shut vault door in front of me. I brush my hands against the door's cold naval pipes and valves. I try to pull on it, but it doesn't budge. I crack my finger to light up the area, and something on the floor catches my eye. I bend down to pick it up, and it's a piece of paper. Scribbled on it are words and poor, hard-to-make-out drawings.

'Janx, I know you are reading this. Only you could be dumb enough to fall through a tree. I built this hideout close to your house when you were a baby. I was a close friend of your parents, and I had to watch you when they left. I can't let anyone see what's in here, so I had to seal it shut. They're coming, and I have to repair the door before they take me. Do NOT come looking for me. -Reez'

I throw the paper onto the ground, cracking my finger again to turn the light off, and I trudge up the dirt slide. I crawl on all fours, my hands splashing little puddles of mud on my way up. I reach the tree opening, and I throw myself through it. I land on the grass, my face staring at the dark, cloudy sky. I sit up, looking toward the dirty back of the nightclub. A strike of purple lightning hits the ground next to me, burning a patch of land. I stand up, lumbering into the streets of Lükahmp.

I walk into the Lükahmp nightclub; the dark lighting and flashing neon lights paint the rooms. I walk through crowds of dancers, drinkers, and downers until I reach the back bar. A purple Zargon in a black suit walks up to me as I take a seat. It sets down a brown cracked glass bottle of Streamo. I take a sip of the Streamo and feel the familiar sweet, honey-like taste hit my tongue, although it's dull this time. I swallow and set the bottle down on the hardwood counter as I see something sit next to me from the corner of my eye.

"You are hard to track sometimes," he says. 'He' being Marz. I turn to him, seeing his familiar scared face. His eyepatch is gone, and I can see his foggy white eye rolling around in his head.

"You are hard to believe sometimes," I say back. Marz slightly turns his head but retracts it after. "There's a reason Al-X is so hated, isn't there?"

"Of course, many people have lost their mone-" Marz starts, and I slam my fist on the table, which Marz reacts to.

"I'm not talking about the money, you monkey," I say, my voice rising in volume. Marz pauses for a moment.

"He's misunderstood, and I'm trying to protect him. He is the key to divine life. That revolution hates him because they want to think they're important."

"He went as far as to obliterate my house just because he lost a woman," I say back. "Killed innocents in a restaurant for no reason. You're lying, Marz. You have been the whole time."

Marz turns to face me, and his other eye trembles. He tries to speak, but I scoot closer to him.

"Either tell me the truth or tell me where Reez is," I say, pulling a double-decker pistol out from my corset. I point it straight at his heart, and he stares at it. He slowly pans his eyes to meet mine as his arm buzzes the table. I watch as he slowly wipes his arm like I do, and a similar hologram appears from his hand. He reads something that I cannot see, and a smile forms on his furry face.

"Prince Gewarsh is a client of mine, and he supports Al-X to the extreme. I give him survivors of any attack that I command. But, of course, in order to get to him, you must get into his fortress," Marz says. He holds his hand in front of my face, and the hologram glitches into a poster for a dance. "Luckily for you, he's having a little dance tomorrow, and I can get you free access."

"How can I trust you?" I ask. I push the edge of the pistol into his stomach.

"You can't," he responds. "But at least you can see your friend again."

~~

Such a lovely community.

A city of inbred six-armed freaks with the anatomy of homosapiens and the features of arachnids. Such a waste of Gellax's pure universal energy. The only entrance left open is the most unstable…and prone to falling down.

Magona stands before the smoldering lift in the center of Arthropodia. Speckles of ash and smoking chunks of dirt float down from the ground above. He stands with the orange sword in his hands, the blade barely an inch off the floor below him. The weapon's edges burst with orange light, and sparks of red energy erupt around the hilt. As the lift crumbles, Magona rotates to view the falling city around him.

The dirt houses are now dark red, with the dancing flames growing in the area. Magona's wrinkled, pale face watches with milky gray eyes as the fire cast an orange light over him. He can feel the slight pressure of rising energy levels in the space around him, tugging at his aging skin.

"Do you know what you are doing?" a voice echoes from beyond the flames. Magona almost loosens his grip on the handle as he sees a familiar face emerge from the fire before him.

"Death?" Magona calls out to his old ally. An aged, piss-yellow skeleton donning mangled brown fabric around its neck stands ahead of Magona's sweating person. "I don't need redemption anymore."

"You'll still get it. Even if you manage to enact your plan to the end, some kink will steer everything off course," Death explains. The flames wiggle across the dirt, almost wholly swallowing Death in its hot grasp. The skeleton stands still as his bones darken and the cloth burns away.

"You are so sure of everything... aren't you?" Magona calls out. "I should just strike you down and make sure you FINALLY leave my side."

Magona raises his sword and points the sparkling blade's end to Death. The fires on the elder skeleton rage on as he places both bony hands onto the orange metal. His fingers melt into the blade, and a crack forms where the pieces are all placed back together. Magona stands shocked, trying to rip the sword from Death's grip.

"This is a dangerous game you are playing, Magona. Nothing good will come of it, ok?" Death finally whispers. He lets go of the blade, the ends of his fingers charred from the orange energy. "Your plan WILL backfire."

With these words, Death steps backward, into the furious flames and smoke, out of view. Magona lowers his fractured sword to his side, the blade's sparks of light growing more violent. He hears the sound of footsteps around him as he sees black hooded figures run amok the ruins of Arthropodia, aiding each other in clearing the surrounding inferno.

~The Ball~

After I left the nightclub, I picked out the fanciest outfit. An elegant black ball gown that stretches down to my ankles. Puffy gray spheres line the bottom of the dress, and a gray fox pelt lies across my shoulders. A small cut on the right side of the skirt lets my bruised leg shine through the gown. Long black gloves cover my arm, from my hand to my elbow.

Contrary to the princess-like dress I have on, my footwear is my usual knee-high boots with three-inch heels. The shoes have white bleached laces on the front that criss-cross from top to bottom. I put my hair in a messy bun earlier, with two strands flowing down my face. To match the dress, I applied black lipstick and eyeshadow.

In order to get to the fortress of Gewarsh, I had to hitch a ride from Marz in the back of a transport hover vehicle. On the way, he showed me the map layout of the castle, telling me where Reez could be.

"Listen, you need to sneak into the back halls and find the empty storage rooms," he says to me.

"Why are you doing this?" I ask.

"What do you mean?" Marz asks back, and I look at him.

"Taking me right to someone who opposes you and the almighty Al-X," I say. Marz turns his head to look out of the tiny slit in the transport walls.

"At this point, even if you find out the truth, you can kill me and everyone connected to Al-X, but you won't be able to stop him."

I don't speak for the rest of the ride. Eventually, it comes to a slow stop. The back of the transport opens into a ramp, which I walk down. I hold my dress up as I step in front of the fortress.

Prince Gewarsh's four-story castle is unbelievable. The white pillars that surround the outside, the marble walls and roof, and the large colorful stained glass windows. They all depict the Life of Madam Loca, a tall tale that the planet believes. Large green poles with circular lights line the metal fencing around the property. A large gate in front of the central garden is open, letting the wealthy of Loca come in for the party. I step through the gates as the other guests stare at my glistering attire. They all seem to line up around me, almost like I'm walking a red carpet to the front door. I walk up the massive amount of stairs and past the pillars right up to the small wooden doors. I raise my hand to knock, but they open before my skin touches the door.

Before me stands Prince Gewarsh in all his glory, wearing a white sailor's suit, but decked out in a golden trim and diamond buttons. His face has a cleanly shaven beard, yellow slicked-back hair, a curved nose, and teal eyes. He stretches his mouth into a smile that shows off his snowy teeth. He grabs my hand with his hairy hands and pulls me into the building, right into the ballroom. A large, circular room with a high roof, a windowed dome on the ceiling, narrow windows on the walls, and a table with a giant white and pink cake surrounded by drinks and frosted cupcakes in the middle of the dance floor.

Gewarsh spins me around as he brings me to the other groups and couples slow dancing as the slow, melodic melody of Count Me My Dollar Double by Sacred Braids begins to crawl through the air. I feel myself pushed away as the Prince walks over to the door to greet another lonely woman. Once he's out of my sight, I move through the crowds of dancers to the door that leads right into the rest of the house. Along the way, I take one of the beer bottles from the table, drink it in one gulp, and set the empty bottle on top of someone's waiter tray. I look around to see if anyone's watching, but everyone's too busy drinking and having fun to notice. I open the door just enough to squeeze through, then close it behind me.

I'm greeted by a dark hallway with fresh white wallpaper and the smell of rotten meat. The only light source is from the fifth moon of Loca, Sermarina, which shines a soft pink through the large windows on either side of the hall. On the wall opposite me, four black metal doors face me. Each one has a tile in the middle with a number; it goes one, two, three, five. I walk up to the first door, seeing a keyhole underneath a shiny golden doorknob. I bow down to look through, my dress restricting my movement. On the other side of the room, I see a dim room with a hanging body in the middle, chained to the ceiling by its arms. It seems to be a Gharbleen, a short, plump, green creature with fat purple lips, wide pointed ears, and a bald, bubbly head. They rule under the Gharbleen King on the seventh moon of Loca, named Kat-Obarp.

This one's nude, with shredded skin around its crotch. The periwinkle-colored blood drips down into a steel pan on the ground, which is already overflowing. Its chest is adorned in bloody slashes and minor cuts along his chained wrists. I move away from the door, moving across the wall to door two.

I can see a few bodies lying on the floor through the keyhole. Then, without taking my eyes off, I slide my hand up the door until it touches the doorknob. I turn it until I feel the door move forward an inch. Then, I step into the room, seeing a bloodied body lying against the wall. The features are hard to make out with all the gore covering them.

Then, I see a familiar face chained up to a steaming pipe in the corner. I run over to Reez, whose head is being cauterized by the pipe. I pick his head up, having to peel it from the tube. I rest my hands on the shoulders of a black jacket with the same logo from the hideout on the sleeves. I close my eyes, thinking I'm too late until I hear him breathing.

"Ree? Oh, thank goodness you're alive!" I yell, wrapping my arms around his battered body. I can feel my heartbeat grow faster. My eyes begin to water as Reez breaks down with his face uncomfortably against my right shoulder. He whimpers a few times as I pat his back. My hands rub across his back through a hole in his jacket. The cuts across his back smear blood all over my hand, but I don't mind.

"J, I…I don't know what happened," Reez begins to cry out as he lifts his head up. "Our base was attacked by Daytör's army, and they wiped out so many of our troops. Are we close to finishing Al-X off?"

I nod, wiping the sweat off my forehead. I can feel my heartbeat return to its average pace. I place my hands on his sides and help him get up.

"Let's get you out of these binds," I say, pulling a knife out of my corset and slapping it against the chain. He shakes his arms and smiles a weak but genuine smile. He wraps his loose arm around me like I did, and this time I lay my head on his shoulder.

I love you.

Reez lets go and lands a small kiss on my forehead. My heartbeat increases again as the chain snaps off his arm. He brushes his bruised hand through my hair as he walks toward the door.

"J, listen. I know we didn't have the best goodbye, but please join the revolution. Don't trust Marz. He is using y-," Reez swiftly turns around and attempts to continue, but his eyes light up. He stands still for a moment before falling forward into my arms.

"Reez? Reez? REEZ? Hey, hey, what's happening?" I ask, slowly lowering him to the ground. The color in his blood-red eyes begins to fade, and the scars around his body begin to bleed again. A tear falls down his cheek.

"They tortured me, J after they took me. Left me to rot in the darkness of some cave. Filled with Mushrumian corpses."

"Reez, what do you mean Mushrumian corpses?" I ask.

"J. Listen. Al-X isn't human. I don't think I can tell you now but find the caves. Get to the Temple of Akur. Find Dhamaneek. Save Loca." Reez turns his head and looks behind me. He slowly removes his jacket, his hands trembling. He wraps it around me, and I put my arms through the sleeves. He smiles, and I smile back. "For everyone but me."

"Ree, I can't go anywhere without you," I say. I let out a small laugh in between the shaking of my lips. He takes another look behind me and laughs a slight chuckle. The color in his eyes fades entirely as he tries to speak. His mouth slowly opens, and I can see the movement of his throat as a splatter of blood shoots into my eyes. I stumble back, wiping my eyes out with my blood-stained fingers.

"Every last one. Marz gave me a simple task at the same time he gave it to you. To kill every single one of those opposing little shits, and you couldn't even kill five?" someone yells. The voice sounds like it's coming from all over the room.

I know that voice.

"Honestly, you had such a good reputation from other employers. They even had you as their favorite, but once Marz became your priority, he used you for his own gain. And you couldn't even kill Julia-N."

Once my vision returns, I blink the rest of the blood out. I look down at Reez, whose left eye is now squirting blood. I turn my head to the door to see it wide open and Ace standing in the doorway. He holds out a small white and blue blaster with a silencer on the end. In his other hand, he holds a decapitated head by its spine. He throws it out in front of me, and a head of a pale, moon-like skinned man, with a long brown beard with hair flowing across his face. A missing nose, with ripped flesh where it should be, beginning between the eyes and returning to flesh above the top lip. Broken sunglasses lodged in one of the eyes. A steel jaw, mold colored.

"I'm gonna be honest, J, I don't know why he had some creature in his bunker, but it seems like it couldn't have been THAT dangerous."

"Ace," I say, my eyebrows scrunching my eyelids down. Ace walks into the light, and his new wardrobe stands out. A black cloak with a symbol on the chest area. A sword shape with an upside-down triangle above it. "How'd you know I would be here?"

"I was up for another job. He told me I'd find you here. Look, I'm not the biggest fan of Al-X, but Magona tells me he's special."

Magona. I've heard that before.

"Who's Magona?" I ask. Ace laughs, keeping his blaster trained on me. From behind, the figure of Prince Gewarsh steps into the light. He dons the same cloak as Ace.

"Our savior who will cleanse the worlds," Prince Gewarsh says. His voice creeps past his lips, almost sliding through my ears. "And we are devoted to him and all he has made."

Ace steps closer, walking toward the steaming pipe behind me. He pats my head with his unarmed hand, the fur feeling stiff against my hair. His fingers push down my scalp, sharp nails cutting through my skin. I scream and close my eyes, trying to punch his arm away. I flail my hands up, but Prince Gewarsh walks over and grabs onto my wrists. I continue wailing, even as my voice cracks.

"Listen, it'll all be over soon. We'll just…remove your brain and let you live the rest of your life without remembering anything," Ace says, his voice twisting into something sinister.

Ace begins to twist his hand around, cutting a circle on the top of my head. I try to move my arms, but Prince Gewarsh keeps his tight grip. Ace almost completes the ring as a booming sound erupts from the ballroom. Screaming and crashing follow. The boys look back as the door to the main hall bursts open, with four soldiers running in. They all hold similar blasters to Ace's but with extended magazines and flashlights attached to the sides. Their wardrobes are all the same; purple and yellow striped body armor wrapped around their body with an unknown sticky residue. Their heavy orange pants and boots clash with the rest of the outfit but somehow work. Two of the soldiers have on circular black helmets with a different symbol than the destroyed hideout. A simple gray checkmark with two purple lines behind it.

The other two have their one unique masks. The first soldier, who's currently grabbing onto Prince Gewarsh and slamming him against the wall, has on a half helmet. It only covers the front half of his head and leaves a long cloud of white hair streaming down his back. The front of the mask has a dark purple visor over the eyes and neon green lines painted over the helmet. The second soldier, who's currently blasting bullets into Ace's back and slicing his hand off with an extending blade from her foot, has an all-around mask. It's painted dark brown and has a visor, albeit dark green instead of purple. Miniature paintings of flowers made of bloody fingerprints decorate the edges of the helmet.

"Janx? How the fuck did you get here?" the white hair soldier asks, removing the detached hand from my head. I can't speak due to high blood loss. I feel like I'm detaching from my body as I'm hoisted over one of the twin soldier's shoulders. I'm carried out into the mess of a ballroom, with corpses and blood lining the floors. I look back to see the two unique guards stomping the life out of Prince Gewarsh and Ace until their faces are one with the ground. A chandelier falls from the ceiling, crushing a breathing guest. I feel like I'm watching my body be brought out instead of being myself.

They bring me outside, back into the gardens, where a beefy star system traveler awaits. I'm not keen on the different kinds, but this one is a purple and orange heavily modified D16-Crack Tiger. It's a wide trapezoid shape, with little legs for support underneath. A small door opens down to provide a ramp at the more extensive base of the trapezoid. I'm hauled on board and into a small room with rows of gray beds and one door on the far wall. Keypads, rectangular lights, and fancy shelves decorate the blinding white walls. I'm laid down on a bed in the corner and propped up against the cold wall. The two twin soldiers walk through the door, which slides in the wall as they pass through. It closes as the unique soldiers walk up the ramp.

"Who are you? More people here to kidnap me? Just end my life at this point," I say. Blood leaks down my face, pooling at the bottom of my eyes. The white-haired character grabs onto his mask with both hands, pulling it off his head, revealing dark skin and a bony, malnourished shape.

"Janx, where have you been?" he asks. It's the man from the restaurant.

"Have you even told her your name? She needs to know everyone that helped Reez," the other soldier asks as they press some buttons on a keypad that brings up the ramp. They remove their helmet to reveal Juwles in all her leafy glory.

"The name's Tyre," the white-haired man says. He attempts a fake smile, but I don't react. "I'm sorry about Reez. But right now, we need to treat that."

He points to my bloody scalp, which is almost disconnected from the rest of my head. Juwles walks to one of the fancy shelves, picking up some small white bottles. She hands them to Tyre, who puts them on the bed next to me as he prepares a procedure.

~The Mistake~

"Is everything ok?" Tyre asks, applying some sort of liquid to my head. I don't respond. Instead, I pull Reez's jacket over my cold body. I rest my head against the wall of the aircraft. I pull out something from an inside pocket. It's a patch with the same symbol from Reez's hideout; a red half circle beneath two black exes on a light blue background.

"Janx, we're going to take you to our base and get you all settled down, ok?" Juwles says from the corner of the room; I don't respond to her either. I put the patch back in the pocket and close my eyes.

"Let's just leave her be, for now. It's been a rough few days for her. She'll recover quickly," I hear Tyre whisper to Juwles.

"You're gonna put her through the plan still? We need her to trust us, not think she's some test subject. Reez died for us, so we co-," Juwles begins.

"Excuse me?" Tyre cuts in, his voice louder than before. "Died for US? What are you talking about? His death was in vain; he wasn't KIA. He was going to carry out this mission, and now we have her."

"When we started this thing, you said that every death was for the greater good. Correct? That every death meant something?"

I peek one eye open to see Tyre staring at Juwles, looking extremely disappointed. Juwles stands with one hand on her forehead, pacing around the room.

"His death means we shouldn't go through with it. We need to trust Dhamaneek. Reez did, so we should too," Juwles says, finally standing still. Tyre sighs and looks off into space. He shakes his head, walking through the door into another room. Juwles curses under her breath as she walks toward me. I quickly close my eye as I feel her sit next to me.

"Hey, J," she whispers. I pretend to wake up, fake yawning. "We're bringing you to our little hideout, and don't worry, this one's more secretive."

"Good," I respond. My head still feels off, and the top of my scalp pulses in a circle. "How different is this ship? Is it really that modified?

"Yeah, this ship has been modified using basically all Tyre's money," Juwles explains. "He made sure to have a shell crafted from solidified decelerated electromagnetic radiation so we can pass through SVE fields. Most planets have a fine atmosphere with adequate SVE radiation levels, but planets like Roan have varying amounts."

"It can travel off-planet?" I ask. Juwles nods. "Could you just take me to Inaz?"

"That farming planet near Roan?" Juwles asks. I nod back. "I would love to, but…."
Juwles looks at the closed door next to us.

"He's in control now that Reez is gone."

"Is that bad?" I ask. Juwles looks back at me and smiles; a few leaves fall off her face.

"No, we just don't get along sometimes."

The door opens, and Tyre steps out, walking to the

keypad and lowering the ramp. A harsh, golden light shines in.

"We're here," he says, walking down the ramp into a cloud of cheering. Juwles stands up and follows behind, walking into the light. I try to move, but one of the twin soldiers emerges from the door and holds a hand.

"Don't. I got you," he says in a deep voice. He slides his arms under me and carries me off the bed, through the room, and down the ramp. My eyes adjust to the light, and I see the D16 is surrounded by a few dozen creatures. They all cheer as Tyre walks through them, giving them all high-fives and hugs. The area around us is inside some cave, with purple and orange vines and flowers twirling around the stones. A fruity, almost floral smell glides through the air.

"I see everyone's happy!" Tyre yells. The crowd silences as he speaks. "But we have distressing news. Al-X has ordered an attack on Big R's hideout, and he won. We have no survivors from the attack, but we tracked down their bodies and found someone."

He turns to me, and so does the crowd. They all stare at my dirty, bleeding body as I stay cuddled in Reez's jacket.

"She will be nursed back to health, and then we will lead the revolution in the name of Reez!"

The crowd cheers and jumps up as I see Juwles stand sternly in the back. She stares at Tyre with murderous intent. My carrier turns around and begins walking over a short wooden bridge covering a deep purple river. The bridge leads to white rooms that stick out from the rock walls, with a gray metal door, like the one in the D16. I'm brought through the door and met by a few Aerans. Deep sea creatures with droopy cheek fins, jagged gills across their necks, webbed fingers and toes, and a slimy body. These ones all wear dirty orange overalls and gloves, along with compact goggles over their eyes. Their gills move as their clammy skin leaks water.

They pick me up from the soldier's arms, who walks back out into the crowd. The Aerans carry me through a blinding white hallway into yet another empty walled room. They lay me down on a bed that I cannot see and poke needles into my arms. I feel blood rush out one arm, and something else rushes into another as my eyes give way.

—

"Mayor Eroper, how will you address the corruption of Al-X and his casino?" a heavenly voice asks.

"Well, I believe that it's the people that are corrupt. Not the Al-X," a stuffed voice says in response. My eyes open and shoot to a hanging hologram display in the left corner of the room. A live interview of Mayor Eroper plays, and it pauses as Tyre walks into the room through an open doorway. He still wears his soldier outfit from earlier.

"That," he says, pointing at the Mayor. "Is Al-X."

"What?" I ask, still being very out of my head. Tyre steps past the doorway, and the door closes behind him.

"Al-X killed the Mayor of Carishem. Doesn't it make sense? At one point, he was against gambling and throwing money out, and he was skinny. And then he went missing, and when he came back, he was fat and loved the casino. So it only makes sense."

"TYRE!" someone yells from outside the room. "OPEN THIS DAMN DOOR NOW!"

"Janx, believe me. You need to come with me and kill Al-X and help Loca," Tyre says, walking closer to me and getting in my face. He takes the orange shard from his pocket and slides it into my jacket. An impact folds the door in half and falls to the ground. Juwles walks through and slaps Tyre in the face as he tries to leave past her.

"My room. Now," she says. Tyre's skin turns a lighter shade as Juwles grabs onto his right ear and pulls him out of the room into the hallway. I look back at the interview as it begins to play.

"Now, Mayor, if you don't mind. Do you plan on addressing any of the controversies about these so-called revolutions being brewed?"

"I will squash them all like the bugs they are. And Al-X will remain safe. Goodnight, Carishem, you sleepy town."

———

After some time lying down, my head slowly recuperates. The needles pull blood slowly close up, and so do the tubes with the unknown liquid. I carefully sit up, examining my beaten body. I look at my wrists, which are mahogany red and indented from Gewarsh's grip. My hands slightly tremble as I move them around. My left side is moderately bruised and bloody, while my right is still charred and wrinkled, a dark nougat color with visible black veins. Reez's jacket is folded at the edge of the bed, next to my legs. My melted corset had been peeled off my skin, judging by the patches of ripped skin around my right breast. Even my leggings are gone, and my bare right leg looks like the skin melted right onto the bones. A soft, thin baby blue blanket covers my left half, which I pull over to shelter the rest of my body.

I lay back down as the door to the room opens, and a bulky purple machine walks in. It has a humanoid shape, in a sense. The legs are robotic and made of heavy metal plates that envelop wires. The body is a T shape, with the arms coming out from the waist. They end in elongated, sharp fingers that hang down like the arms. In the middle of the chest is some sort of octagonal window, with a spinning orange light on the other side. The head looks like a lopsided rectangle with two linen-colored horns on the side.

A large, painted grin reaches both sides of the face. Above the mouth are two large red circles, with six other small deep blue orbs around them. A small hole opens at the very top of the head, and a little platform is raised up. A highly tiny four-inch tall man sits on top of it. His arms are stretched out to two little levers next to him. I can barely determine his appearance as he pulls the switches to move the robot to my right. It moves almost squatly, with the legs always bent and keeping the upper body as still as possible. The painted mouth opens up to a speaker behind it.

"Hello, Jan X," it says.

"Janx, actually," I correct it.

"Apologies. I am Row-N, creator of my Leathean Machines. I also excel in medicine. I was going to pick you up from that restaurant a few days ago, but you were missing when I got there. Tyre was there; he said you left."

The robot's low arms move the blanket off my body's right, and the head awkwardly moves lower to examine my burns. It holds up my right arm, looking at the black veins.

"You have severe blood clotting; many layers of tissue are basically nonexistent; I'm surprised you're still alive."

"If I'm still alive and seemingly fine, what's there to heal?" I ask. The machine's head turns to me and stares into my eyes.

"Half of your body looks like a popped testicle. I can at least fix some of the missing muscle tissue, but your skin will still look charred."

Row-N retracts his platform into the head of the robot, and the opening closes. The robot lowers my arm onto the bed and turns around, walking through the smooth white wall. I lay confused as it phases through again, holding some sort of needle gun. It has a handle connected to a long needle, with a tube of pink liquid. He holds up my arm once more and slowly inserts the needle into my black veins, filling each one. The black is gradually overcome by blue blood again. I can feel my control over my arm slowly come back to me.

Once the tube is empty, the robot unscrews it off the back of the handle and crushes it in its hand. Then, the particles of glass fizzle through his fingers onto the ground. His sizeable left eye opens, and another tube pops out. Next, he catches it midair and screws it into the needle gun. This time, the tube contains coral-colored liquid. Finally, he sticks the needle into random areas of my right arm, leg, and chest. The skin expands almost back to normal but is still charred and slightly yellow.

"And there you go. I told you I excelled in medicine. I created all of this just for the revolution. Can't have the government taking it from us," Row-N laughs from inside the robot. "You're good to leave."

The machine stomps out of the room, and I sit up, grabbing the jacket. I attempt to throw it over my back but decide to tie it around my exposed lower half. I twist off the bed, my bare feet hitting the hard tile ground. I walk a few steps, my legs shaking as I regain my balance. I hear the interview playing in the room's corner as I walk through the door. Then, past the door, I choose to walk left out into a large clearing.

I find myself on the other side of the giant mountain base and in an endless vanilla-tinted field. The light from outside takes a second to get used to, and the turquoise sunrise is a sight to sore eyes. I look behind me to see the mountainous settlement with the singular entrance door I emerged from.

"Hey!" someone calls out. I see a soldier in familiar armor running up to me from a tower in the distance. I hold my arms over my chest as I approach him. He slows his run, panting as he bends over to catch his breath.

"You aren't supposed to be in the open like this during flyby hours," he says, his words spread apart with heavy deep breaths. "Come on."

He turns around and begins to slowly trek back to the stone tower. I join him, walking toward the three-story tall building made of prismarine-colored stones and a dark brown wooden door. Next, we walk through the vanilla fields, through the grains of Zlar berries. Finally, we reach the tower, which seemed more prominent than the mountains. The soldier opens the wooden door into a circular room with a few goons on black boxes around a gray table. On top is a bright orange box with a small light in the middle that displays a video hologram, the only light source in the room.

"What are you watching?" I ask one of the soldiers, who's holding a handful of smashed Zlar berries. He points to the hologram as he puts some Zlar in his mouth.

"Just some archive footage of Al-X," he says, chewing very loudly.

"Turn it up."

The soldier slides a greasy finger on the bottom of the projector, and the volume increases.

"-ishem. This revolution…will be met with something greater than themselves. I will squash them all

like the bugs they are. And my casino will remain safe.
Goodnight Carishem, you sleepy town. End of message."

"Where's Tyre?" I quickly ask. The sleepy soldier
slowly looks in my direction.

"He's uh…in the meeting room. In his D16, I
think," he says. I run out of the tower, through the vanilla
grass, past the blinding hallways, over the bridge, to the
landing pad where the D16 waits. The purple vines and
flowers give way as I bolt over them, leaping up the ramp
into the bed-filled chamber. I run toward the door into the
mysterious other room.

"Tyre. You're right," I say, bursting through the
doorway. I see Juwles pointing a finger at Tyre, who's
holding himself in a lounge chair behind a wooden desk.
Around the walls are brown metal shelves filled with
bottles of liquids. A singular yellow light bulb hangs from
the ceiling, and a wide slit of a window displays the
outside.

"Janx!" Juwles exclaims. She grabs a pair of heavy
orange pants from atop the table and throws them at me.
"Put some pants on!"

"Right," I say, catching them. I put my legs
through and untie the jacket around my waist. I slide my
arms through the sleeves, and I zipper the front. "I need to
talk to Tyre about Mayor Eroper."

"See, Juwles? I'm right," Tyre says, puffing his
chest out as he stands up from the chair. Juwles shakes her
head and walks past us into the bed row room.

"There were similar speeches from Al-X and the

mayor, and you might be right," I say to Tyre, who smiles.

"When have I ever been wrong?" he says back.

"Tyre, you have five minutes," Juwles says as she walks down the ramp. She picks up a stone from the ground and throws it into the purple river. She turns around as she begins to speak. "And she's staying."

"What?" Tyre says as he slams his fists into the keypad, bringing up the ramp and smashing the console. "We're ending this, Juwles. Now."

"TYRE!" Juwles yells from beyond the door. Her screams are fizzled out as the ramp closes. Tyre flashes a quick smile at me, walking into the main room. I try to follow, but the door closes behind him and won't open for me. I bang my bruised arms on it.

"Hey, I can't get through!" I yell. "Tyre?"

I hear no response, only the crackling sound of the engines meets my ears. I run over to the ramp, where I can see the mountain base shrinking as we travel away from it through a small crack in the side. I slowly approach one of the beds, laying down on it as I regret everything.

—

"We're here," Tyre says, finally coming out of his chamber. The D16 jolts with the impact of the ground. "Look, I know I kinda just kidnapped you twice in the past few hours, but we do not have much time. We must kill Al-X as soon as we can."

"WHY?" I yell at him, quickly sitting up on the bed. "This is just a circle of death, destruction, and getting nothing done. 'Let's kill Al-X. We can kill him this time!

Oh, he's so bad!' Why, Tyre? What length will you go for this?"

Tyre's smile fades sooner than I could finish my sentence.

"I joined this revolution because I was friends with Reez and because Al-X slaughtered most of my family. They were in debt to Al-X, and he ordered Lord Daytör to kill them all. He spared me because I was only a child. I spent my whole life looking for them, to get revenge. I even tracked them to Roan, where I found the shard. The only one who was left was my sister. For only a week."

He grabs his mask from the back of his waist and puts it on.

"And now Al-X is more powerful than before, and Daytör searches for it."

He walks over to me, grabs onto my wrists like Prince Gewarsh did, and pulls me off the bed. I crash onto the ground, and Tyre shoves something in my face. I look at it to see a small vial with a sludgy black goo.

"This came from Juwles' laboratory. She didn't want me taking it. I thought that we could use you somehow. To see what the shard selected you for, but it seems like you're nothing. So this is our last hope," he says, shoving the tube in my face. The goo shakes around as he does. He grabs my burnt hand, pressing the vile into my charred skin and pushing my fingers over it. The pain strikes my whole body, and I hold back tears as he pulls me to the ramp by my bad arm. I'm dragged along the ground and kicked down the ramp into a patch of moist grass.

"Tyre, please," I try to plead. He ignores me and waits for me to stand up. I slowly push myself to my feet, being greeted by the back side of Al-X's casino. I look around, past the D16, to see the backsides of other clean, shiny buildings.

"Easy landing spot for drug trades, but also access to the ventilation," Tyre says. He crouches down at the base of the casino, feeling around the yellow bricks. His fingers sink into a part of it, and he nods in satisfaction. "It's here."

He pushes his fingers into the wall and pulls off a chunk of fake bricks. He scatters them around behind him, revealing a small hole of darkness. He stands up and pushes me toward it.

"He should be on the top floor. Do you have the vile?" he asks. I nod. "Good. When you see him, open it and let the goo crawl to him. Now, go."

I crouch down, looking back at Tyre, who flashes a quick fake smile. I nod back at him, sliding myself into the dusty vent entrance. I crawl on my stomach, pulling myself forward with my dirty hands. Every sound makes a seemingly endless echo.

I make my way through the air duct maze, checking my map every few seconds to ensure I'm going the right way. I get a few yards away from the entrance as I realize one of the paths leads to a meeting room.

"Tyre," I say into my earpiece.

"What?" he asks back, the mic cracking.

"Could I check to see if he's in the meeting place?" I ask. I wait for a response.

"You can check," Tyre finally responds.

"Roger," I say, continuing my way through.

—

I reach the meeting room ducts, and midway through, there's a hole that lets in the room's light. I look through the small cracks in the side into the expansive meeting room. Positioned in the middle of the room is a long black wooden table, surrounded by fifteen figures. Though most are hard to make out, I can see Hail Lēy, Al-X, and some other mayors of Loca. But, of course, the Mayor of Carishem is missing, and Al-X is wearing his face mask of Valure Eroper, much to everyone's unknowingness. On the opposite side of the room is a large window displaying the houses of Carishem.

He's also dressed in a fancy black suit, which is very clean and reflects the light off like freshly wiped glass. His small framed glasses sit crooked on his face. His teeth are still yellow and hole-filled as a sponge. He stands at the front of the table, speaking to his fellow authority. I take the vile with the parasite, popping the top off and throwing it into the room.

Al-X begins sweating, messing around with his notecards as he stutters more and more. The other mayors don't seem to notice, and Hail Lēy is sleeping on the other side of the table. Al-X continues to say his speech until he drops all his cards while trying to flip to the next one. He curses as he bends over to pick them up.

I can see the minuscule parasite crawl along the ground under the table, latching onto the bottom of one of the cards. Al-X picks them up, apologizing and continuing his statement. He starts talking about something important, creating some discussion around the table. A smile emerges from his crusty face, which is short-lived as I can see him grow uncomfortable.

Minor sweat stains start to spread under his arms, and dark circles form around his eyes. A pool of saliva seeps from the corner of his mouth. Al-X removes his suit jacket, which is now drenched in sweat. Even his undershirt is wetter than a Locanagwan marsh. He continues to stutter and has trouble speaking his words. After a few notecards full of confusing sentences, one of the mayors stands up. She walks over to Al-X and places a hand on his shoulder. They say something to each other, but I can't hear it.

Al-X seems to be in some pain but tries to hide it. He unbuttons the top button on his shirt, revealing a large patch of hair. He then walks over to the table, places down the notecards, and removes his tie. He reassures the room that he is fine, and they all look at each other with unease. They grow worried as Al-X's pants begin to darken, starting from the crotch.

He removes his belt, which drops his pants onto the floor around his ankles. He starts groaning in pain as his white underwear soaks in sweat. He falls forward, shooting his hands onto the table to stop his descent. All the mayors jump out of their chairs, except the mystery woman and

Hail Lēy, who is still sleeping. They all run through the small glass door on the side of the room.

The woman walks behind Al-X, placing her hand on his back again. He starts choking, spit flying onto the table surface. He reacts to some sharp pain, covering his crotch with his hands and notecards. Then, I move my head closer to the gap for a better look. He begins to yell louder, and I can see the bulge in his underwear grow, ripping the bottom of the cloth. He falls onto the ground, lying in a puddle of his own sweat.

Al-X grabs onto the ripped edges, pulling them completely off. His testicles and extremely short dick are exposed. The wrinkled, hairy gonads continue to expand, precisely like a balloon. He grabs onto them, still holding the notecards, trying to stop the enlargement. He starts to scream even louder, and sweat drenches his entire body. He scratches at his hairy berries, making them bleed with the force. The woman slowly backs toward the door, tapping on Hail Lēy's back. Al-X's testicles stop growing, ending at the size of two adult human heads; he stops screaming but continues to groan in extreme pain.

Suddenly, the skin on his nards begins to squirm around, like something is underneath. I slowly push the broken vent pieces to slightly peek my head even closer than before. I see Al-X lift his head up to examine the mess when a loud pop sound kills my eardrums. I roll backward, covering my ears and trying to drown out the ringing. I wince in pain as I can feel blood dripping from my earlobe.

I slowly lower my hands from my ears, rolling back to view Al-X. He's totally knocked out. I look down at his crotch to see a head. A fat, pale head poking out from the popped scrotum, covered in blood, hair, and chunks of furrowed skin. The head begins to slide out of the hole, moving through the slippery blood-covered floor.

The entire creature crawls out and stands up, precisely what Tyre described it as looking like. A chubby fetus thing, with two broad black eyes, a forever open void for a mouth, and no arms. A blood-covered umbilical cord hangs from a bleeding hole in its stomach. It makes humanoid baby sounds, sounding slightly off, almost like a robot. It waddles away from Al-X's body, who wakes up to see what he just birthed, only to faint again.

The woman backs into the corner next to the exit door, slowly sliding down the wall. She's in tears, screaming as the little fetus wobbles toward her. It turns when it moves, putting one side in front of the other. The baby noises continue to emerge from the child. It stops in between the woman's outstretched legs, going quiet.

She lowers her arms in front of her face, believing the baby to be peaceful. She laughs as she looks at it, seeing the somewhat cute face of the demonic entity. Her tears become tears of happiness. Her eyebrows raise. She reaches out to pick up the child, raising it in front of her face.

Something is said to the fetus, but I'm still too far away to hear. The woman laughs as she holds the thing closer to her face. The armless infant makes an echoey baby laugh as it headbutts the woman in the face. She drops the newborn onto the ground, and it hits the carpet floor and bounces for a second. The woman's nose is streaming with blood.

She tries to kick the creature, but it steps out of the way. With her eyes closed and both hands over her nose, the woman tries to roll away. The fetus slowly waddles and follows her, where it catches up and bites the woman in the spine through the clothing and muscle. She screams, slamming her hand onto the ground and keeps its grip on her backbone, slowly pulling it out.

The woman's head slowly flattens as the entire upper skeleton is gruesomely pulled out. The intestines drop from the ribs as it's brought into the outside world. The demon lets go of the spine, letting it fall onto the ground. Blood streams from the back incision. The child walks away through the gap in the glass exit door. During the entire ordeal, I was too stunned to speak.

"The whole building is in lockdown. Some guards are coming toward me, so I have to leave you in there," I hear Tyre say over the transceiver. From beyond the vent, I can hear screaming echo through. I also hear the creaking of a door opening. I open my map to see the fastest route as my legs are grabbed from behind. I try to look, but I am yanked out and thrown onto the bloody, feces-enveloped meeting room floor.

All sorts of bodily fluids and dismembered chunks are crushed as my back slams against the long table. I feel a fragment of the side crack off with the force. Above me are three Dice Bots; one with one eye, one with three eyes, and Snake Eyes himself. Snake Eyes' left-hand floats over to my mouth and covers it as the other hovers over me, holding a needle. I try to fight back, pulling at the hand over my mouth. It keeps its position as the other hand slowly pokes the needle into a visible vein in my throat, breaking the skin and oozing something into my bloodstream.

My vision is blotted out as I can see the Dice Bots lift me up, carrying me along with the body of Al-X.

—

I wake up, still not being able to see. My legs and arms are held together with something cold, which matches the freezing, moist floor I'm laid on. I shoot my body up, but I land on my other side. Whispers start to wrap around me.

"Is she ok?" a high-pitched voice says.

"How did she fall?" a more resounding one booms.

"Can you see?" a closer one asks.

"No, where am I?" I cry out. The darkness and lack of sight continue to horrify me as I can feel soft fingers trickle down my unmovable arms. The fingers multiply as they grasp onto the skin. I'm pulled up by my restricted arms, letting me struggle to stand up on my own.

The whispers continue as a clamorous slam comes from behind me. I turn around for no reason, still blind. All the fingers let go of me, and new pairs of hands latch onto me. At the same time, I can hear nine distinct screams of terror. I'm pulled forward and dragged through the icy room into a warmer area.

As we are brought into the next room, my vision partially restores. Although very blurry, I can see the nine women, all of different species and races, and all dressed in either dirty rags or nothing. We're all chained around our ankles and hands by rusty shackles. Notably, however, one of the women is dressed in a fancy pink and white dress, which stands out. Her skin is a light brown, with fluffy black hair poofing down to her neck.

The circular room itself is still very out of focus, but colors of white, gold, and neon mix together. Two Dice Bots are on my side and the other women's sides. Their detached hands hold onto everyone's arms, pulling them into the middle of the warm chamber. Sweat begins to stream down my forehead. I blink a few times, trying to bring back my sight. Windows along the walls shine in the light, which blinds my eyes.

After a moment of waiting, the wall across from me lifts up, leading to a large hall of blurry stone statues, large golden-paned windows that bleed through golden beams, and chiseled pillars that hold up the tall ceiling. The walls stretch up into a shining golden void. My vision finally comes to.

There are eight sculptures, four on either side of the room. Each one is Al-X in different poses, such as standing nude holding a cup or naked holding a skull over his crotch. The floor is lined with a red and black carpet, extending to stairs on the other side of the room. The stairs lead to a throne with a rebar frame covered in dismembered human baby hands. The cushions are just a pile of nude posters.

And, of course, Al-X is sitting on top of the greasy throne, wearing nothing. His oily scrotum is on full display, held together by poor stitches and tons of needles. The skin itself is very outstretched and empty. All the girls, including me, are pushed into the middle of the room, forming a straight line across. The Dice Bots all let go of our arms yet stay at our side. Some of the girls have teary eyes and horrified faces but remain silent.
"How pretty you all are…but I can only choose one," Al-X says, his greasy breath reaching my nose from so far away. "Such nice, smooth bodies…."

"Whose children are those?" one of the women asks. Al-X looks around at his chair, and his grin grows wider.

"Mine. Child organs are…so valuable. If you know where to sell. And I need them quickly…, so I choose a new woman every few months to be my bearer," he says. We all stand horrified at his explanation. "And one of you will be mine."

"Why are you doing this?" another woman asks, this one balling her eyes out.
"Loca is corrupt. And I plan on making everyone scared of me so that I can become more divine than I already am," Al-X explains. "Now, onward with the choosing. You, I want you to strip."

He points to a woman in a pink dress with dark skin and hairy arms. Some of the Dice Bots approach him as he takes a step forward. She lifts her arms up, pulling at the chains. She's able to break them with her strength, and all of the Dice Bots hover and block Al-X's body. The woman grabs the dress's collar, ripping it down the middle. It takes a while, but she eventually tears it entirely off. Underneath is nothing but skin and freshly shaved male genitalia.

What the hell?

"My name is Demeon, and I have come to send my ANGER!" he yells out, his voice now intense and masculine. He bends over and slams his fists onto the binds around his ankles, breaking them as well. He lowers his eyebrows and opens his mouth, yelling as he runs across the hall, dodging every Dice Bot. He jumps up the stairs, floating in front of Al-X.

"This is for the people of Loca!" he yells. He extends his leg out, kicking Al-X square in his chubby nose. The man yells again in victory as he shoots himself out of the window on Al-X's right. The sound of him continuing to victory scream slowly drowns out as he runs through the Carishem towns. Al-X pushes his glasses back up his nose, wiping some blood off in the process.

"You. I recognize you," he says, pointing to me. My eyes widen as two guards walk over to me, grabbing onto my arms. I try to wiggle out, but their grip is too tight. "Strip."

"NO," I yell out as the Dice Bots grab onto the top of my jacket. They pull down on it, ripping part of the sleeves. They hold onto my pants, tearing the cloth into pieces, exposing my half-burnt legs. They push me onto my stomach, and I try to stop the fall with my shackled arms, but they are just crushed under my breasts. All around me are the remains of my clothing, and Al-X cheers as I look up at him, my face completely red.

"It's you! Such a wonderful body...ever since I saw you in that restaurant. I hoped that we could meet again," he says, almost singing the words. "You will make a fabulous wife and live the rest of your life with me."

He motions at the Dice Bots with his hands, and they grab onto my naked body, lifting me up and dragging me along the ground toward Al-X. My bare feet scratch the carpet with my nails. I try to wiggle out and scream to be let go, but the Dice Bots don't budge. They carry my almost-limp body up the stairs, and I'm thrown onto the raised floor in front of the reeking throne. Al-X smiles with his yellow teeth shining extra golden. He stands up, towering over me. His shadow freezes my body where it touches. I notice his eyes are slightly yellow and a bit bloodshot.

"What shall we do with the other women?" one of the Dice Bots says from below. Al-X peeks over me and looks at the line of people. He thinks for a moment.

"The buyers should be here tomorrow morning. Tell them the quality is undecided, and we're down one. Bring them back to the cave in the meantime."

The women all scream, pleading for their lives as the Dice Bots pull them away, through the open wall, back into the moist chamber. The cries are silenced as the wall closes behind them. I stare in horror at the wall, which holds a long painting of Al-X at a table along with nine other people.

One of whom is Marz.

~The Auction~

The nine buyers step into the room. Each has a small tag on their clothing with their name written in purple ink. They all walk across the red carpet, sitting on one of nine chairs spread out in the room. In order, they all introduce themselves.

The first, Klebar, is a tan Phroug. They're tall creatures that have an upside-down arch shape. The legs connect at the top with the body, and large white eyes are embedded into the flesh. Their feet are blocky stones made of bundled dead skin. Under the arch is the mouth, which hangs down from a long tube. Fleshly wires are strewn all over the creature. Klebar's wearing an elegant black two-piece suit wrapped around his legs and a velvet purple hat.

The second, Majson, is one of Row-N's Leathean Machines. His blocky shape, long brown human hair, and a manufactured face make his appearance uncanny. He's all gray, with the exception of his natural faded brown hair, and his eyes and mouth glow a bright blue. He doesn't have expressions, but he is still imposing.

The third, Cyree, is a big-eyed, buck tooth Travish with dark blue skin. Large slits in his exposed, moist chest allow him to breathe above water. His face consists of two pearl eyes looking in separate directions, little fins around his ears, and two whisker-like appendages sticking out above his little mouth. His blue body has yellow patterns all around, like birthmarks. He dons only a black skirt, which reaches to his webbed feet.

The fourth, Nojhor, is a lavender cobblestone monster. Atop a trunk of crumbling rock sits a cross-shaped gravestone with three green crystal eyes along the middle. Two lengthy legs extend from the sides of the torso, slowly dragging along the ground as the creature moves along.

The fifth, Ahshh, is a yellow-haired barbarian with a long beard that dangles from his pronounced chin. A wide unibrow hovers over his thin, squinting, misty green eyes. Only a loincloth, boots made of Zargon scales, and a backpack cover his body. The muscular, tattoo-covered, trimmed chest stands out next to the sizeable double-sided battle ax held in his hand. Dark scars glide across his chiseled arms, almost like tribal paint.

The sixth, Tuck, is a dark yellow-skinned human with a similar body to Al-X; a big build with a lot of fat underneath his gray robes. His face is elongated and thin, looking flat from the front. His eyes are on either side, and his lips bulge out from his face. He wears a black cloak, similar to the one Ace was wearing at the ball, complete with the same sword-like symbol.

The seventh, Baree, is a silhouette of negative energy. I can make out the figure of a human-like creature, but the form of the being is like a mirror of everything around it. The only difference being the reflections are all monotone, backward, and show all events in reverse. I can see the mirroring of him purchasing a young green animal of an unknown race as, in the present time, he sits amongst the others.

The eighth, Maa Bribe, walks in, also sporting a black cloak but has the hood over his head. Both arms are crossed, with the hands in the sleeves. He sits on his chair, removing his hood to reveal long, curly golden hair atop a skeletal pink face. Veins bulge from the base of his neck, disappearing underneath his robes. Large, circular silver eyes and two pincers on the sides of his mouth give him a bug face.

And the ninth, a familiar one. Marz enters last, wearing a spiky black leather jacket and denim shorts. He dons a new scar right above his chin, which seems to be from something of high temperature. The furry skin around the cut is now bubbly and wrinkled, the wound almost yellow in color.

"What happened to you?" Al-X asks from his throne. Chained by my ankles, I'm forced to stand next to him.

"Daytör is not pleased with the breaches of security, sir," Marz responds as he sits formally in his chair. "I had to tell him about our little run-in at the Prince's house."

"Fair enough. Tell him it will be dealt with…in our own ways," Al-X says, blinking at Marz. "Anyway, let us begin with the auction. We have eight beautiful women for you all today."

"Eight? There's usually way more than that!" Tuck yells out in a deep raspy voice. He shakes a fist in the air as he complains. "We're not going to accept this!"

"I understand your disappointment, but…we have

had some runners. More than usual," Al-X explains. "Even right before you all arrived, we had one escape."

"Tighten your security, you scaramouche," Ahshh says. Al-X quickly spins his head in the direction of Ahshh, his flabby cheeks wiggling in the process.

"Excuse me?" Al-X asks. His eyebrows lower, and he points at Ahshh. I can see a few Dice Bots appear from behind the statues. "Wait a minute…you look different."

"What are you talking about? I've been coming to these for years," Ahshh begins to spurt out.

"No, no, no," Al-X cuts in. "What's on your neck, Ahshh?"

A Dice Bot hovers over to Ahshh and grabs onto his head, pushing it down and revealing an inky black tattoo on Ahshh's neck. It's of some sort of symbol, but the distance blurs it into a dark circle. The Dice Bot lets go, and Ahshh's head violently snaps into position.

"Magona will fall, and so will you. Reez will be avenged," Ahshh yells out.

"Ahshh…I want you to lay down at the bottom stair," Al-X says, pointing at him. Ahshh hesitantly stands from his chair, walking to the first step. He slowly bends one knee as two Dice Bots approach from behind and slam him onto the ground. The edge of the step cuts his forehead; yellow blood seeping from the wound. "Now, open your mouth and bite the edge."

As Ahshh opens his trembling lips and envelops the stair, Al-X slowly walks down to him. He stands over Ahshh, with both feet next to Ahshh's head. Ahshh flinches with every slight movement as his teeth grind against the hard concrete. Al-X's moldy toes wiggle around as he stands proud in front of the other eight buyers.

"Let this be a message to you all if you so choose to disobey Magona," he says. He smiles as he raises his right leg. He slams it down on Ahshh's head, his teeth curving into his mouth and the edges of his cheeks ripping apart. The yellow blood drips down the step onto the red carpet. Al-X raises and drops his foot again, Ahshh's cheeks pulling farther until his jaw disconnects from the head. The teeth break off and drop onto the ground, clinking as they hit the concrete. Al-X bends over and pulls the top two-thirds of Ahshh's head off, holding it out. He kicks the rest of the body, and it rolls to Tuck's feet.

"And now…we begin," Al-X says again. He turns to me and places a fat hand on my bruised cheek, rubbing it with a thumb. "We can't spoil your surprise, dear."

As he finishes his sentence, his grip on my face tightens, and he throws me down the carpeted stairs. My head knocks into one of the steps, and I black out as I feel my chains pull me back.

———

The sounds of shuffling and metal clanking together brings me back to reality. I can feel cold air around me and something breathing near my legs.

"Hello, Janx!" Marz says as I open my eyes. A ringing in my ears drown out his voice. "Such a funny thing…seeing you here in my abode."

"What the fuck is wrong with you? I thought I was done with you," I yell out at him. Marz walks around the sepia-colored room, with bookcases, shelves, and dressers dotted around the walls. The short ceiling is appropriate for the height of Marz, and the bed I find myself bound to is also properly stubby. My legs hang off poles at the edge of the sheets. The only light is from a singular lit candle atop a tall brown nightstand in the far right corner. The whole room smells similar to the pine trees imported from Earth, and most importantly, Reez's jacket hangs on the wall above my head.

"I must say, you still have an attitude unlike anyone I know," Marz responds. "Don't worry, I have no plans to hurt you or anything…immoral."

"You bought me?" I realize. I try to lunge at Marz from the bed, but the shackles restrict my movement. He chuckles, and I look down at my wrinkled right arm. I can move it more freely around the cuff than on my left.

"Well, you are a valued product for my…new master, Lord Magona. He has seen your commitment to your craft, Lordess Janx," Marz says. I scoff at the new title.

"I am a Lordess, now?" I say most sarcastically. Marz smiles and nods.

"Amongst the underground Cult of Magona, you are indeed a celebrity," Marz explains. "Lord Magona believes you are the key to unlocking the ancient Temple of Akur."

"I'm the key?" I ask.

"He can sense something in you…an almost mystical power. He knows where the temple is. It's located in the winding maze that is the Mushrumian caves. He was there, just in the shadows."

My mind flashes to when I exited the caves and saw that imitating dark figure with the unforgetful white mask. How I left all of those Mushrumians to be slaughtered by the Cult. As my memory continues and the sounds of the Stoean ocean ripple through my ears, the same chime of the waves flows through the room, mixing with the ringing.

"We're in Stoean?" I ask.

"Of course. I had to make sure you were as close as possible," Marz responds. "And soon, Lord Magona will come here to transport you himself!"

Marz turns to face an oil painting on the wall of an older-looking Marz, one with long, gray hair and a cracked monocle over their right eye. I take this time to pull my right arm against the cuff. The harsh, disheveled metal ring pierces into the furrowed skin, little fragments chipping off my wrist. The hand doesn't even bleed, much to my confusion. Eventually, enough skin is ripped away, lining the bedsheets under the cuff, and I can slip the arm out. Looking around the room, I search for an escape and a plan.

"My greatest grandfather, the one that began this family, was one of Magona's first believers," Marz begins to say. "One of the pure-races that we all hope to keep in check."

I grab onto a shredded hardback book from the dresser on my right, throwing it at the back of Marz's head. He falls to the ground, dark gray blood seeping from a newly acquired cut on his skin. I drag my left arm out of the chains, removing the binds on my legs. Marz wipes the back of his head as he stumbles onto his feet. He grabs onto the edge of the bed and turns to face me; the ringing stops.

His face droops as I look upon a hole in his forehead. I sit up to look down at where he fell, to see a shattered mug covered in gray fluids. I look back to Marz, whose hole displays part of his aged yellow skeleton, ripped pink muscle, and chunks of orange brain plopping onto the bedsheets.

"Marz?" I say, holding out a hand to him for support. He stares at me for a prolonged amount of time before collapsing and slamming against the hardwood floor. I hop off the bed, seeing the corpse of Marz lying flat on the ground next to the mug fragment and thrown book. All I can think about is the suddenness of it all.

Grabbing the jacket from the wall and some dirty pants underneath the bed, I make my way out of the room. Right before I exit through the door, I look down to the thrown book. Yellow papers spill out across the bloodstained ground, with crime scene photos paperclipped to them. I lean down to check them out, seeing a familiar sight.

The photos are of the night Ace, and I murdered Whensdaie Minoim during a job for Marz. We found out after that Al-X had killed the rest of the family, which meant Whensdaie's brother was without supervision. By the time I went back for him, he was gone.

I throw the photos back onto the ground and continue on my way. I walk into an industrial staircase with metal steps and wire handrails. It leads into darkness, but I opt to traverse upward toward a light pink light.

Through a chipped brown wooden door, I stumble into the beach of Stoean, seeing the familiar green sand. I walk toward the Mushrumian caves, letting the blue ocean wash the blood from my feet. The blinding sun sets in the distance, the sky being a pink and yellow mix. I stop as I reach the broken platform. The metal plate dangles from the pulley, hanging over the sand connected to a little post sticking up from the ground. I look down at the twelve and a half miles of void as I take a deep breath. I carefully put my foot on the platform's edge and grab onto the rope. My weight gradually lowers the metal, bringing me down into the caves.

At the bottom, I jump off before the platform touches the ground. I'm at a lower level than where I was last time. This time, the caves are light gray, with no signs of growing Mushrumians in the walls. I see slashes from a sword across all of the walls, scorching the stones. I crack my finger, which glows as I light up my path.

"Let's hope I can find what Reez wanted me to see," I say to myself, beginning my walk into the cave system.

—

Eventually, the gray walls begin to morph into green stone and rock. The floor evens out, as does the ceiling. Torches start to adorn the walls, to which I turn off my finger light. Then, they give off a soft, yellow glow that clears the darkness. Then, after the cave walls fully transform, two towering figures appear from a distance. They both are giant skeletons, seemingly made of brown and green wood. Capes dangle from their neck, shredded cloth covered in purple flowers and vines. I turn around to walk back to the platform, but I'm met with a green stone wall.

"Do not fear, my child," a heavenly voice calls from behind. I turn to see the two wooden skeletons standing around a man. He has a cyborg lower half and a robotic right eye. His human upper chest is extremely buff, almost ripping out of the stained white shirt he has on. His right arm is just a stump, contrasting his complex left arm. The edge is also a stump, but it's adorned with wires and metal plates that connect to an arm made of thin steel and human veins wrapped around them. His beefy neck is topped off with a plump face and curly black hair. His mouth breaks into a smile that squints his large, circular yellow eyes.

"Is this a temple?" I ask, backing up into the wall. The man steps forward, smiling larger than before.

"Yes, you are at the Temple of Akur. I am glad you found it, Janx; we have been waiting for you."

"You know me?" I ask, slowly retracting from the wall. He nods.

"Reez came down here a lot. He did start the revolution after all. He would always tell us about you." The man whispers something to both of the skeletons, and they walk back into the distance. "Come, come, we have a lot to talk about."

"How can I trust you?"

"This is for you," he says, pulling a weathered book from his shirt. He hands it to me, and I quickly take it from him. I look at the brown leather cover, examining the letters. 'Reez's Logs of The Light.' I open to random parts of the book, seeing scribbles and ramblings throughout the pages.

"He wanted you to have this when he first met you. When you were ready, of course. You and I are the only two living beings to know about this, so keep it secret," the man says. "Not even Dhamaneek knows."

My ears perk up.

"Reez told me to talk to him. I remember. Before he…died," I say to him. Reez's smile flashes in my head for a moment. The man's smile fades.

"Yeah, I found out the hard way. I could feel it. A shift in the weather, almost," he says, his voice slowing. "Anyway, you just need to continue on your path, and you'll reach the doors. And don't mind the skeletons; they're only guards. Nice to meet you, Janx."

He turns around and walks away, and I shove the book into one of my back pants pockets. I pick my head up, and I journey to the temple.

—

I reach the Temple of Akur's doors; large wooden double planks adorned with vines and purple bearded irises warping from the cracks. I push on both doors, and they slowly creak inward. Soft yellow light shines as the two ascending guards cross their staffs over me. I walk through a seemingly endless hall of shelves filled with books; each shelf reaches high into the ceiling, disappearing into the darkness. They're wooden with steel legs supporting them. In the middle of the hall is an extended clearing, with a red carpet across the floor. I see a few creatures walking throughout the temple, flipping through the dusty books. Behind me, the doors slam shut, shaking the room.

"Excuse me, how may I help you?" I hear. The voice sounds masculine yet slightly squeaky. From one of the shelves on the left, a tall yet plump creature walks out, with long aquamarine fingers interlocked across its chest. The beast is around my height, maybe an inch or two shorter. The bottom of the neck begins about two feet high, and its head is almost at the same height as mine, albeit with a longer, square chin. The dark, black eyes and droopy nose are at the very top of its head, and its perked mouth is in the middle. A black bowl cut matches the black beard it dons. The bulging, veiny, two-and-a-half-foot tall neck extends into the square body, with two stubby legs barely supporting his weight. Contrasting to his long, skinny fingers, his arms are barely half a foot long.

"Yes, I was told to come here by an old…friend," I respond. "I wasn't told what I'm looking for, just that I need to talk to Dhamaneek."

"That is I," the creature says. "And who sent you?"

"Reez-N," I say, taking out his patch from my jacket pocket. Dhamaneek reaches a hand out and takes the patch with his disturbing fingers. He examines it, looking at each little crevice and loose string.

"How's that old hag doing? I've known him for longer than he's had fur on his ass!" Dhamaneek laughs, handing the patch back to me. He notices my lips droop down like his nose. "Is he safe? Is he alright?"

"He told me to come here. It was the last thing he said," I tell him. His cheerful expression slowly matches my grim mood. We both stand, looking at the ground, not making a sound.

"Did he tell you why you had to come here?" Dhamaneek finally asks, breaking the silence. "Is he still part of his little revolution group?"

"Yes, and I just recently joined. For him."

"Then you know about Al-X?" Dhamaneek asks.

"Just a bit, but it all combines into confusing knowledge," I respond. He nods his head and walks away, past the shelves of books. I quickly follow behind him.

"I will explain to you what Reez spent his life keeping secret and what he devoted his work to. What you will do with this information is out of our discretion. With Reez now dead, the temple is open to the public. I exist only to provide history."

~~

"Sir," Maa Bribe says, his voice clicking with each

word. He kneels on the red carpet leading up to Al-X's throne. He bows his bug-face, the golden light reflecting off his pink skin; his pincers dance around his drooling mouth.

"Yes, Mr. Bribe?" Al-X booms from atop his rebar and baby arm throne. His legs are spread wide open, letting the light wind blow across the remains of his hairy popped nutsacks; taped around the insides of his legs. "Have you found something for me?"

"Sir, I have just returned from Marz's hideout," Maa responds. "We have a breach."

"I let Marz take that woman…because he thinks he could hide their ties from me," Al-X laughs. He claps his meaty hands together as he stands up from his chair. "And where is she to now?"

"Sir, I watched her enter the Mushrumian caves. Any idea why?" Maa asks. Al-X's joyful expression dims as he processes what he hears.

"The Mushrumian caves?" Al-X asks for clarity. Maa nods his head. "What lies down there is none of your concern. Thank you for the information, but I will have to act on it now."

"Yes, sir," Maa says, standing up only to bow. When he straightens, he turns and exits the room as two Dice Bots violently pull a hunk of metal along. Al-X raises an eyebrow in curiosity.

"And who is this?" Al-X asks as the robot is thrown to the bottom stair. Al-X begins to walk down toward it slowly.

"Al-X, sir, we found him lurking about Carishem looking for a woman," one of the Dice Bots says. "Janx is the name."

"And what could he want with her?" Al-X rhetorically asks. He stands next to the fallen purple robot, admiring the T shape of the body; dented metal plates that cover exposed wires, all joining together in the middle to shelter an orange core. Eight red circles blink on its head, a few shattered from the fall.

"Name?" Al-X asks. He leans over and puts a hand behind his ear. The robot's mouth opens up to reveal a speaker behind it.

"Row-N," he responds. "Creator of th-"

"The Leathean Machines," Al-X finishes. "Yeah, never been a fan."

"Where is Janx?" Row-N asks. "Just let her go…you can have me."

"Oh, I already let her go," Al-X laughs. He looks over at the Dice Bots, which join in his laughter. "She's in the Mushrumian caves right now…and I'm about to join her."

"You won't be able to get into the temple, Divine," Row-N says as Al-X turns his back on him. Al-X goes up one stair and stops, not looking back. "Don't think I don't know what I was getting myself into here."

"Dice Bots, send him to Treenun," Al-X says. He spins one of his fingers in the air, and both Dice Bots grab onto Row-N's broad mechanical shoulders. Then, they drag him along the carpet, black oil spilling onto it.

"YOU CAN'T RUN FROM MAGONA," Row-N yells out as he's pulled out of the room. When Al-X is alone, he walks to his throne and slams his fist into the middle. The rebar cuts along his knuckles, yet he doesn't flinch. Al-X sits back in his chair, tilting his head and waiting for an opportunity.

~The History~

We enter a room through a door on the right side of the hall. It's dark, with the only light coming from a window in the ceiling. It lets in the moonlight from the night sky through a hole that reaches all the way to the surface. The round walls surround a map of the planet etched into the ground. It has a date written on the bottom right-hand corner, but it's hard to make out. Dhamaneek slides his fingers across the walls, and they light up, showing images of war, famine, and death.

"The story I am about to tell you will be long but will help you to understand how to kill Al-X," he explains.

"If the information is so easily available down here, then how come nobody has gotten close to killing him?" I ask.

"You'll soon learn he is not human, and Reez made sure to keep this temple secret. For good reason."

The images on the walls merge together into one of space. An image of a planet appears on the farthest point from the entrance door. It's bright green and dark blue, with lights covering the land matching the surrounding stars.

"Earth I was a planet; a planet full of thousands of sentient beings; all different races."

As Dhamaneek speaks, the images shift to what he's talking about.

"Humans, as you may know them, were a very, VERY, idiotic race, and still are. There were only around fifteen human beings during this time, and they were the least populated race on Earth I. The planet began with advanced buildings, and even the humans were intelligent. The most intellectually advanced race was the Keeblins.

They had large brains with six lobes: the frontal, the parietal, the temporal, the occipital, the acutal, and the malignal lobes. The acutal was a small area on top of the frontal lobe that helped with the complex eyesight that the Keblins had, and the malignal lobe could detect any danger throughout the body. It was helpful because it could find harmful bacteria in other people's bloodstreams by just touching their blood.

While the Keblins were the dominant race and they oversaw the rest of Earth I, they were also incredibly egotistical and wished to be the 'gods' of their home. Keeblins also developed a religion to The Seven Hellbringers, and they called it Sevrinchístt. The Seven Hellbringers was the group of seven lords of unreachable power, and Lord Sparaky believed that he was approached by the Lord of the Stars in a dream.

The following morning, he sent his follower Adam, a fellow Keblin, to search for the Lord of the Stars. After years of waiting, the resources of Earth I began to deplete. In response, Lord Sparaky rallied the population together and sent a distress signal to the farthest corners of the universe. They were found by the Cult of Magona, a group you may be familiar with."

I nod my head as he continues.

"The cult brought them to a planet almost identical

to Earth I, that was recently discovered to be nonpopulated. They called it Earth II. According to the writings of Adam, nearly days after they arrived on Earth II, Lord Sparaky's stomach burst with the light of a thousand suns. The skin flowed through the air like fabric in the wind as a ball of energy hovered from the belly. Lord Sparaky's body became deflated as the orb grew in size, sinking down toward the garden grass. It phased through the ground, leaving the sight of all who witnessed it. Everyone stood in disbelief as the sky lit up and the people's spirits lifted. Even Lord Sparaky's stomach closed up, the light dimming away. They all would live as they did on Earth I, praising the new orb of light that lived on the Earth as The Divine. All the species came together in their new home, building it into castles and a society.

All would be well until the humans began to grow in numbers. Their population outnumbered the Keblins within months, and they were scared. The other species feared the new dominant race, so they planned to overthrow the Keblins. Lord Sparaky was even threatened by Adam, who built the Garden of Eden along with his peer Eve. They wanted to force the Keblins to build for them due to their intellect and previous infrastructure knowledge. Slavery was born.

The humans kept the Keblins and every other insufficient non-humanoid race as servants for their every bidding. They kept them in underground tombs and catacombs, chained together, forcing them to stay in the darkness for hours until they were needed. On Earth I, crossbreeding was forbidden. After humans became the prominent species, they disobeyed the rule, and thus, crossbreeding brought animals. This lasted for seven thousand years, when one day, Eve was approached by a wild snake in Adam's garden on an apple tree.

'The apple...a Keblin'sss biggessst weaknesssss. One sssniff of these and they do anything...' the snake spoke. It wrapped its tail around one singular apple, one that almost spoke to Eve with whispers coming from all around. Eve didn't hesitate as she took the apple, biting into its side. The skies darkened as the teeth touched each other through the pulp, and the ground shook. The snake morphed into a creature of lava that scolded Eve for taking the fruit.

The monster chained all humans down to the Earth with the arms of the damned, letting the trapped species in the deep underground free. They all escaped into the bleeding skies, finding a way to escape from the now treacherous land of Earth II. The humans remained confined to the land as they starved for weeks. After eight weeks, they were freed from the grasps and scrambled to return to their old selves. All humans tried to regroup but failed as the cracks in the land broke into seven continents. Life continued from there, although much slower and less advanced.

By the time Sevrinchístt began to fizzle from the words of the humans, The Divine awoke from its slumber and created the creature The Sacred, a beast of no appearance that only takes the form of what The Divine decides. During the rise of Eden's Garden II, The Sacred took the form of a man with long hair and sandy robes. He walked across deserts and water, hoping to scare the humans into leaving Earth II and leaving it to The Divine. However, the humans decided to praise the being, creating a religion around him. While most believed in him, thinking of him as the Son of one true God, others accepted him as the upbringing of Death himself.

The Divine sent up four of his ascending guards: Mathew, Mark, Luke, and Johhn. He sent them up to watch and record the Sacred's actions. They separated their works into the Old and New testament. The Old was written without mentioning their names to avoid being tracked down during The Sacred's reign. After the death of the Son at the hands of the Romans, the four ascending guards wrote the New Testament, this time using their names as the fear of discovery was at an end. They had the books copied and delivered throughout the religious groups of Earth II. Most declined, but those who took the books either followed the preachings or twisted them into their own ideas.

Now, these religions slowly spread across the galaxy with scavengers, travelers, and even dictators visiting Earth II. They would hear the words of the humans and take them back to their own worlds; thus, religion became important. Some even stayed on Earth II and spread their own ideologies. However, the answer you are seeking about Al-X is almost unknown. There is only one story that we have on file. And it's from Reez himself. He is nearly as old as the planet itself, older than even Al-X. It is dated within the first ten thousand years of Loca's existence and gives details about The Divine and how it works. He talks about his experience mining deep into the planet, finding colonies of creatures living close to the core. They were mostly molten, being able to sustain the increasingly hot temperatures. So, one day while working almost feet away from the center, wearing the same heat protective suits that we do today, an orb of light came to him. According to our records, this was around the same time Earth II was discovered and populated.

It came to Reez, passed through him, and entered the core of Loca. Light flooded the underground caves, and the area around the core broke and stone formed into the Temple of Akur that you are standing in. After his vision was restored and the light faded, he approached the temple and watched as The Divine, which he named himself, sat in the same place the core did before. He also watched as Al-X was born right before his eyes, fading into existence.

He tried to frighten Reez, who stood in awe. He ran up the caves to tell his people, who all thought Al-X was sent from the gods. You see, everyone on Loca was Sevrinchíst before Earth II's spread of religions. From here on, Al-X's rise to power is documented in other texts but always begins from his birth as a child, which never happened. It's also good to note how each documentary about him is paid for by Al-X himself."

"So Al-X is some sort of extraterrestrial being?" I ask. Dhamaneek nods.

"He is of an otherworldly energy, one with levels that we aren't able to document," he says. "We hope that someone can find a way to stop him with our knowledge, but I do not think it's possible."

"And you said that the orb came here? Did it just live in the walls of this temple?" I ask. Dhamaneek laughs, covering his mouth with his foot-long fingers.

"Yes, we still have the chamber it lived in, but to visit, you must drop down a pit. Nobody's ever come back from it," he says. He opens the dark history room door and walks back into the bookshelf hallway. It's less populated than before, and I count about three creatures roaming. "I will show you the main chamber, however."

We begin walking down the hall, and as we walk, a slight shake knocks some books over. I exchange glances with Dhamaneek, who seems a little confused. He looks around for a moment before continuing to walk. Then, as we get further into the temple, the shelves are farther apart, and the books appear taller.

"Why are these books bigger?" I ask.

"They get older as we get closer to the middle. Our writing and alphabet have definitely changed over the past thousand years," Dhamaneek explains. "Some of these are even in languages that are forever lost outside these few books."

In the distance, I see an archway that leads into a dimly lit room. Around the arch are carvings that look as old as the planet. They depict some sort of war, one that I don't seem to recognize. As we pass under the arch, another shake happens, more significant than the first.

"There might be some renovation in the upper caves, nothing to worry about," Dhamaneek reassures me. We enter the large chamber, a domed-shaped room made of green rocks held together by dirt and moss. A large circular opening leads down into darkness in the middle of the stone floor. "This is the pit."

As we get closer to the opening, four figures materialize around it. They all look like the temple guards, with skeleton-like bodies. These ones, however, are only a floating upper body. Their molten black skulls contort on the top, flowing around like flames. Their hanging jaws touch the top of their ribcage, with ribs that end in sharp points. The spine continues past but ends a few inches under the ribs. Their right arms begin in bone, then contort into a tube of orange liquid. Three of them hold onto long staffs made of solidified magma. The fourth one is unarmed. It walks over the pit toward me.

"Greetings, young one," it says. Its voice cracks and echoes in my head. "What brings you to the chamber of The Divine?"

"I am showing her aro-," Dhamaneek starts, and I cut him off.

"I want to jump down," I say. The four guards and Dhamaneek all stare me down. "I want to see what's down there. It could help."

"Listen, my child, The Divine's pit is dangerous, and you won't make it back. Besides, there is nothing down there," the guard responds back. When he finishes speaking, there is another shake. This one is longer and feels closer.

"What is that?" Dhamaneek asks from behind me. The shake stops, then starts again, with a crumbling sound coming from above. Dhamaneek walks to where the sound is the loudest as something crashes through the ceiling. I jump backward, out of the way of falling debris. Dhamaneek is crushed as the object crashes into the stone temple floor.

I wipe dirt off my face as I stand back up, looking at the giant machine lodged into the ground. It's a bulky collage of parts from other planets, all poorly welded together. The front view is of a large, white, truck-like hood, sitting on top of a thin sheet of silver metal that acts as an undercarriage for the vehicle. Broken red and white headlights and sharp brown lead pipes decorate the two tubes on either side of the hood. Only one gray tire supports the front, slightly off to the left side, next to an unknown black box. The vehicle's main body has a window in the front, which is currently shielded by smoke. Above the window is a long stick with a carrot dangling from the end, over the hood. The top of the rod also connects to a wire that feeds into the top of the vehicle.

I walk a little to my right to see the side. The machine extends back into a flatbed with some red painted wooden planks sticking up like a fence. Above is a yellow crane with a blue hook, albeit a plastic model. There's only one door on the vehicle, and it's on the left side. It's a typical white house door, with a doorknob and a pane of glass welded over a large cutout in the middle of the wood. Judging on the placement of the hinges, it looks like the door opens into the car.

Under the flatbed, two black wheels on both sides compensate for the one in the front. A little tube in the back lets out black smoke, which rises into the hole that the vehicle came from. The door opens inward, and a shadowy figure takes up the whole space inside. It attempts to walk out, trying to pull itself through the door frame. The walls of the car compress and crush as it pushes its hands against them. The character finally jumps out of the vehicle, the glow from the hole lighting him up from behind.

"I'm finally home…," Al-X says, the front of his body still shaded in darkness. I can tell he is still naked, and his testicles are still taped together. "I caught wind you were coming here, so I tracked you. Tracked you back to my home. Where I was born."

"You were made by that ball of light. That sat in that chamber," I say as I point to the pit.

"I was created by that ball of light, yes. But to me, it looked different. It was an orb of flesh, with just an eye of blue to watch the world. It sat, imitating the core of the planet to keep it alive. It made me to rid this place of life. To wipe the land of people," Al-X explains, pacing around the room.

"The Divine believes all people are evil and that our future ends in destruction. Eventually, its own plan failed; nobody was afraid. Sure, they're scared, but not enough to leave. I even became acquaintances with beings as twisted as me. I got emotions. I became real. I grew an empire, a following, a business. The Divine became an itch that I had to scratch. It tried to talk to me through my head. I silenced it. I made it die. I ripped out my own brain, and The Divine imploded beneath the crust. I felt it die. I felt it burn. The planet became cold. The core's heat was erased."

"Then how are we all still alive?" I yell out. Al-X's bloodshot yellow eyes shoot around the room, seeming to not land on anything.

"The energy field around the planet that was created when the core was replaced. It's still here; it cannot be destroyed, just like me. I am flesh made of pure energy. I bleed like you, I feel like you, but I cannot die like you," Al-X says, his veins bulging across his body with each line. "I'm glad we met, Janx."

"Why's that?" I ask. A few ascended guards surround me, holding their staffs toward Al-X. The ends glow orange, and lava drips from the bottom. Al-X looks at each guard, smiling and laughing as they all subtly shake in fear. He tries to speak but is silenced as footsteps echo through the chamber.

"Someone's awake," Al-X whispers. We all look around the dark hall, searching for the source of the sounds. Al-X maniacally laughs, dancing around in a circle as the footsteps grow louder. Then, they stop. The only sound left is the soft kiss of the wind from the pit.

"The Sacred of The Divine has returned once

more," a voice booms from the pit. I step over toward it, looking down at the opening. A red bony hand grabs onto the edge, pulling its body up. I notice the shining suit of inverted white magma-infused metal first. It looks just like war armor from the archway etchings. Spikes protrude from the shoulders, and the chest plate has red lines running down the middle. Its head is a skull, just like the guards. It's soaked in blood, with fleshy mounds in the eye cavities.

"My lord, the Ascended Priest," the four guards say in unison. They all bow as the priest steps in front of Al-X, staring him down with his flesh eyes. Al-X falls to his knees, smiling up at the priest.

"You were forbidden ever since you cut the ties to The Divine. You broke the oath you were born with," the priest says, talking down to Al-X in more ways than one. Al-X's manic expression turns dark, his yellow eyes slowly morphing into dark gray.

"YOU THINK THE DIVINE IS THE VICTIM HERE? I NEVER ASKED TO BE BORN!" Al-X yells, standing up and towering over the priest. "I was created by that ORB OF FLESH and forced to do its pest control. It created a man of pure evil just for me to fit in with the kings and queens of this world. I was forced to live even beyond my life expectancy. I tore that stem out of my head to get away from it. It's gone, and you still protect it."

"You can bicker all you want; it doesn't stop our decision to disconnect you forever," the priest yells back. Al-X's eyebrows angle down as his neck is barraged by growing veins. He starts grunting, blood rushing to his face.

"You still stand by something that doesn't exist anymore. I've made a decision. I'll let you visit him," Al-X screams. He grabs the priest's head with both hands, pushing them together. Cracks form across the priest's skull, breaking under pressure until it is shattered. Al-X's hands slap together as the priest's body clatters against the floor. I gasp in response, and Al-X turns his attention to me. He growls, running at me with full force. I turn to run, but he's too fast. He grabs onto my jacket, pulling me back. He lets go, and I slide across the floor. I try to slow my speed, but I slide right into the pit opening.

My hands shoot up to the edge, and I hold on for my life. Al-X walks to me, the ground booming with each step. I look to see him now towering over me, holding one of the guards by the head. He throws it into the pit, and I watch as it flails its arms as it tumbles into the darkness.

"I thought I could get rid of you," Al-X says to me. He softly places his feet on my hands. "I guess I still am pest control."

He pushes his feet down on my hands, and I scream in pain as I feel the bones cracking. My left pointer finger lights up, illuminating the pit. The walls are made of aquamarine stone, and I notice a line of missing stones leading down. I look back at Al-X, whose crusty smile is the last thing I see as he repeatedly drives his heavy toes into my fingers. This time, the bones crumble under his intense weight. Blood engulfs my hands as they slip off the edge, and I plummet into the darkness.

—

Through my fall, the only light I have is my still-lit finger, which dims as I lose all feeling in my hands. Before I can think about that, I crash onto a rock's edge. It goes straight through my stomach, which bifurcates my spine. I cough up blood as I slowly slide down the dirty boulder. When my body stops, I can feel my hanging hair touch wetness. I can't turn my head or move at all. I'm stuck looking up at the darkness, unable to see anything else. My arms hang at my sides, blood dripping from my shattered fingertips.

Whispers echo through the cavern as a soft blue glow illuminates around me. I feel something moist grab me, pushing me off the rock spire; it slides against my exposed insides, making gross sloshing sounds. I'm carried into a body of water and pulled beneath it into the glowing blue sea. My open eyes burn as the water slides behind my eyes, slicing through the optic nerves. The last thing I feel as the soft blue water fades into darkness once more is each bone breaking and my entire body being pulled apart.

~~

Al-X holds the dismembered head of Dhamaneek in his grubby fingers. Dhamaneek's head is forever frozen in a state of shock; the last face he will ever make. The prismarine walls of the chamber are decorated in splashes of multicolor blood, and so are the sides of his drilling vehicle. He walks through the hall of books, letting Dhamaneek's neck drip onto the ground.

"You seem more naked than I thought," someone says from behind. Al-X violently turns around, accidentally throwing Dhamaneek's head into a shelf, the skull shattering and blood splattering. Al-X sets his sights on a dark-skinned, white-haired, green-eyed warrior wearing a black half mask, with a dark purple visor and neon green lines painted down the helmet.

"Yet another fan of Janx, I'm guessing?" Al-X says. "How'd you even get down here?"

"A big hole in the dirt isn't very normal," he responds. "I am here to kill Janx. I left without telling anyone my plans, so there's no company after me."

"Kill Janx?" Al-X asks. "I beat you to it, pal, and besides, what's a low-life X-Rioter doing looking for an assassin?"

"I found where she was being kept. In an Orugnic's house near the beach of Stoean," the man explains. "Maa Bribe isn't good at being interrogated."

Al-X keeps his composition, besides being scared for the first time in a long while. He stands up straight and holds his hand behind his flabby back, letting his ruined dong hang about.

"So? What's it to you?" Al-X says. The man laughs as he removes his mask to reveal two blinding neon green eyes.

"She was tasked with killing a woman named Whensdaie Minoim…my sister. Right in the safety of my Stoean house," the man responds. "Right after you had Lord Daytör slaughter the rest of my family."

"Tyre Minoim…I thought I remembered you," Al-X says. "They were all in debt besides you two. Your family was all gamblers…but your sister wanted you down a different path. Yet even though she succeeded, you still share one trait with the rest of your pathetic ancestry. You all gamble your life with Al-X."

"This tyranny of your rule will come to an end, Al-X," Tyre says, reaching behind his back only to bring out a long golden sword with a black metal hilt. "First, you, then Janx."

"She's already dead," Al-X says. Tyre ignores him and instead bends slightly over, pointing the blade in Al-X's direction. Al-X stands his ground.

"For my sister…Whensdaie…," Tyre says, slowly starting to charge for Al-X, who doesn't move an inch. "FOR MY FAMILY!"

As Tyre reaches Al-X, Al-X reaches a single hand out, grabbing onto the blade as it nears his chest. He holds onto Tyre's head with his other hand, and together, he rips sword from man. The blade crashes against the ground, clinking with each hit. Tyre's back slams into a bookshelf, and his body splits in half.

Al-X stares at the top half of Tyre, which lies face down next to a few fallen books. One is entirely open, and a dim orange light emits from it. He approaches it, pushing one of Tyre's arms off the pages to see a small drawing of Al-X. The paper in the book begins to wrap around Al-X until he's completely covered and fully immersed.

The hole Al-X had come from begins to fill itself

in; dirt and vines pull alongside each other to block the entrance. Even the pit to The Divine's chamber is covered as the bricks contort and join together over the hole. The Temple of Akur is wholly cut off.

~The Eye~

"Lord Daytör...Lord Dayag has advised me that you have been working with a Rogue?" Magona booms to Daytör, whose face remains invisible from the darkness of his black hood. His robes envelop his kneeling body. He bows his head as he tries to explain himself.

"Sir...I was not aware HE was yours," Daytör tries to say. "And besides...he severed his connection, and now he is but a mere mortal."

"I see...but you overlook the bigger image," Magona says back. He paces around the circular chamber of molten black rock. The orange light from the outside corridor shines upon the cracks on the blade. "Al-X is made of my energy...if he cannot be used for my PLAN, then he is no good to me alive. I must retrieve my creation, and we must continue as planned. I need all the energy I can gather...this planet is a good host for new life."

"Yes, my lord," Daytör quietly responds.

"Where is he now?" Magona demands.

"Last I saw of him; he was tracking someone down into one of your temples," Daytör answers.

"Then I shall engulf every last brick of that place in my seed...," Magona says, sweeping black vines emerging from his hands. "And soon, Loca will be ours, and the universe will be all true-race beings."

~~

Wrappings cover my body, seemingly made of Arachnavoid webbing. I'm reminded of Tyre's base and how I awoke in a similar situation. I float in an endless sea of water, somehow able to breathe. All around me is a void of deep blue; silhouettes of creatures swimming all around me. My fingers try to move apart, but a spongy feeling between them restricts it.

A face appears above me; translucent orange tentacles connecting to two bulbous black orbs and a funky-looking gray brain chamber. The tentacles end in sharp metal patches; red lights flicker through the blue water. The two black orbs blink differently, and thin white circles on either one move around sporadically. The swollen head of the creature sits atop a slimy skeletal chest, with two bulging robust arms moving around my body. It swims around with its tail and a triangular orange fin on its back.

It's a Bo-Telail, a race of underwater medics bred to care for each other since they usually live alone. This one rubs against the burns on my right side. The scars and imperfections retract into my arm, and the color turns from blackened marks to my original peach skin. All the pain I've been used to now fizzles away, and I'm only left with the feeling of the cold water.

"Excuse me, miss, but it seems you have had quite a tumble," the creature says. Its voice distorts in the water, and bubbles form at its tentacle-covered mouth. It grabs onto my arms with its strong hands of three webbed fingers, pulling me to the water's surface, where I bob around. The subtle waves brush against my body, and my head knocks into a rocky surface. From the corners of my eyes, I can see the Bo-Telail climb itself onto a raised dark green platform. It slithers across over to my head, where it grabs onto my cheeks and drags me out of the water.

I'm hauled and delicately thrown against a murky silver metallic fence. The Bo-Telail slides across my outstretched legs.

"How are you feeling?" it asks. My brain feels absent, and the feeling across my body is lacking.

"I...am fine...," I make out. "I should be dead... shouldn't I?"

"Well...you did die. Your back was split open by the impact of a piercing fragment of Ceelist," the creature explains. "It's a mineral that grows like a plant in the deepest sections of a planet."

"And how does that explain how I'm alive?" I ask, waves of water splashing against the platforms we rest on.

"You are fortunate, Janx," the creature says.

"How do you know my name?" I quickly snap. I can see my scarred face in the reflection of its void-like eyes. I see droopy eyelids covering my eyes; a brown pupil on my left and a washed-out, milky orb on my right. The scars and burns that deeply covered my body now blend with the rest of my peachy skin, although the bumps and uneven areas remain. My black hair stiffly creeps down either side of my face; hairs sticking up around my scalp. My cheeks bear heavy scars, as does the space around my eyes. The first time I have seen my face in a long time.

I stare at the creature, neither of us saying a word, the only sound being the echoes of distant conversations and the subtle water splashes around us. The Bo-Telail's tentacle mouth wriggles around as its breathing deepens.

"You must follow me. I cannot provide you answers; only Meiv can do that," it says. "She is our savior; the one we serve. She can help you. She's already done it once."

The Bo-Telail swiftly spins around on its tail and squirms off my legs into the darkness of the gated tunnels. I rest my head on the slimy fence behind me, the green light from beyond it shining upon the emerald walls across the sparkling river.

"He is right, you know," a voice calls from behind. I spin my head to see a figure kneeling behind the fence, a pale, almost transparent woman, staring at me. She holds onto the thin wires with four hands, each with six fingers, Her small, spherical face match with bulbous, lavender-flowing eyes. Dark flashes of amethyst and mauve bubble around the pupil area. The smooth, hairless head is decorated with glowing purple crystals that bulge out of her dome. Her four arms connect to a dress of violet-colored stones that scrape against each other with each movement. She looks all too familiar.

"Why….Do I know you?" I ask. I stumble onto my knees, holding onto the bars with her.

"Janx, we have met before. You just were not…yourself," she says. "My name is Meiv. You were still energy when I found you. And indeed, you are extremely fortunate. You fell onto a formation of Ceelist crystals, and your soul was ripped into the Plane of

Celestial. I was quick enough to be able to reach in and reunite your fading body with your spiritual energy."

"What?" I ask, confused about what I am hearing.

"You were sent to the dimension that flows around all of us, but we cannot see," Meiv explains. "It's a realm of the energy from any soul hapless enough to be combined with the inky sorcery of Magona's vegetation."

"I do not follow…why do you speak of these crystals as if they were plants?" I ask in confusion. Purple lines emerge across Meiv's face, starting from her glowing green eyes.

"They live and breathe as if they were…and they were made from The Divine in order to aid in Magona's plan…," Meiv says. "And I know all about it. I was there when my friend…my sister in crime…was taken by the same element you were almost lost to. I was banished here after a good companion of mine was locked away. And here I have been for ages, where Magona's second Divine creation was made. And only a few years ago, The Divine imploded on itself, and a shockwave hit my body, giving me my…imperfections and beauty."

She points all around her body to the bumps of crystal growing from her white skin.

"Could you help…defeat him?" I ask. "Everything going on the past few days…has been all because of Magona. He made Al-X, and Al-X has ruined everything."

"I wish I could," Meiv says. She places a hand on my right wrinkled cheek through the fence. "But I am only a demiGod and am incapable of any major power. I wanted to save you because…I try to save everyone I can from the Plane. At this point, you'll have to either live with us or travel to the surface and…die all over again."

"But it's still safe up there; I can still get a ride out of here from a friend," I quickly plead. Meiv's face stoops as her gleaming purple face dims, swallowing all the light around. "Right?"

"Janx, you are in the deepest layer of Loca," Meiv says, bringing her hands to her side and standing over me. "Without the core being here anymore…time is shattered. By being down here for only a matter of hours…the world around you has progressed years in advance."

"What?" I yell out. Images of my allies flash in my head as I struggle to find what to say. "You're telling me everyone's dead?"

Meiv wipes her glowing hands against the silver fence, and the bars vaporize and burn away. She reaches out to me and holds onto my arms, pulling me closer. The swirling mix of lavender in her eyes is overtaken by a cloud of darkness. All of the crystals protruding from her dim, and the space around us fades until all that is visible is Meiv.

"If you want to save yourself…find The Eternal Brain…," Meiv says. "Get off this world and travel along the Watcher's Trail."

"The Watcher's Trail? I-I don't know what that is?" I stutter. Meiv raises a hand and places a finger on my forehead. Flashes of lavender light streak through her arms, slithering to her fingers. The cold touch of her nail pierces through my face as images flash through my brain, repeating in a specific order.

Fire and burning, dripping black sludge, an endless sea of water, and a brain in a space of black.

"What do these mean?" I ask while in some sort of trance. "The images…?"

"It's the path…you must follow it if you hope to help. I'm worried Magona can read your mind…since you are a de- a human," Meiv awkwardly says, her words overlapping. "I cannot force you to remain down here…since you do have a job to do."

"And what's that exactly?" I ask. The shards in Meiv's skin pulse with purple light, and the area around us fades back in view. Although, now, it's different than before; instead of a platform next to a peaceful river, we find ourselves in a dilapidated prismarine-colored chamber. Toppled pillar and ceiling chunks line the battered stone floor. Meiv slowly spins me around, and I face a colossal orb of oozing brown flesh.

In the middle of the creature, peeled-back skin and scorch marks surround a vast hole in the being that covers a glass eye. The immense size of the flesh-covered eyeball makes me freeze in place. The creature doesn't move, but the eye inside gazes all around the room. It's shined upon by light from behind the being's position.

"What is this?" I ask, turning back to Meiv, who has disappeared.

"Do not be afraid, my friend. I have been hoping for this day," something says from around the room, the voice seemingly bouncing off the stone walls. "Face me once more…please."

I steadily rotate to face the eye as it sets its pupil on me. The black inner circle expands and shrinks rapidly as the ring of white around it stays stationary.

"The Lover herself."

The voice is definitely coming from the eye.

"I'm sorry, I don't follow," I say.

"Oh, I know you don't. You should know that I took the form of an eye on purpose…I can see someone's future, but not their past."

"Wait, what are you? I thought I was going to find remnants of The Divine…not some bald crystal woman and a meatball," I cut in.

"I am The Divine," the eye growls. Its pupil thins itself and looks like a Felishe's eye. "After my creation severed our ties…I had to take the form of SOMETHING or risk being found."

"By who?"

"By Magona. I don't know what he's capable of anymore… he's too strong."

"But he can be stopped, right? Meiv gave me a path to follow," I say.

"The Watcher's Trail?" The Divine asks. "It's a path of ungoverned planets that leads to The Eternal Brain in the heart of the universe."

"Why would she want me to go there?" I ask. The Divine shuts its eye, the flesh crunching together as it joins over the pupil. "Excuse me? I want an answer."

The Divine doesn't respond, nor does it awake again. Instead, I wait for what feels like minutes, but nothing happens. I stumble around The Divine, finding the source of the light behind it.

In the cracks of the dark prismarine stones, a small orange-lit opening leads to a seemingly endless staircase. Looking up, the steps rise into a small dot of light. I put one bare foot on the bottom stair, and it creaks under my weight. I look around the walls for a handrail, but the stones bear no support.

—

The smell of ash and the crashing sounds of lightning overwhelm me as I emerge into the dark outside light. I'm met with the unfortunate sight of Loca; what used to be a lavishing green and blue planet is now covered in a blanket of darkness. The black ash-soaked ground throbs as dark, leafless trees wriggle around in the dirt. The clouds above bend and contort as the view of space ripples like waves.

The sounds around me consist of the aforementioned lightning, pops of lava bubbles, distant screaming, and a new ringing in my ears. I look down at my hands, which are covered in dirt and grease. I wipe them on the equally dirty pants, not wanting to ruin Reez's jacket.

In the sky, ships and vessels soar through the fractured airspace; white spotlights break through the grainy air. I turn back to see the cellar door I had just emerged from. The decaying brown double doors crumble with the slightest kiss of the wind, and the staircase's walls collapse, blocking the way down.

"Excuse me?" I hear a familiar voice say from behind the entrance. I walk around the mound of dirt the doors were in to see a dark, charred man crouching on the ground. His head is burned and scarred, and where his eyes should be are two black holes. Over his body are shreds and fragments of an orange outfit, now primarily brown and seared. The bare chest and legs beneath are mostly burnt skin, barely hanging onto the exposed bones of the man.

I can see a heart dangling in the middle of his torso, held onto by a few rogue veins. It beats slowly, little droplets of lava splashing against the lower ribs. The ends of his arms and neck are the most intact part of his body, and bright orange capillaries can be seen flowing through. Large frowning lips stretch from both cheeks on the man's dark salmon face.

"Blaze?" I ask. The man jumps up, feeling around the air, trying to find me.

"Yes, yes!" he yells out. "That is me! Your voice…so familiar!"

"Yes, I helped you in Arthropodia," I tell him. I move a little closer, letting him find one of my shoulders. He pats me and then lowers his arms.

"Janx…was it?" he says in a quieter voice. "Juwles told me about you."

"What happened? Last time we met, you had eyes," I say. He shrugs down and falls onto his ass. I slowly take a seat next to him.

"He used me...to burn it to the ground," Blaze says. "Fuck...I had to watch as I hurt all of those beings that helped me back to my feet."

"You...killed them?" I say, slightly backing away.

"No, no, no, no," Blaze says, shaking his head violently. "It was moments after you left. He stormed the city and stabbed them with his sword. They just...evaporated into thin air."

He snaps his fingers.

"Like that. And he found me...and he knew what I could be used for. So he threatened me with my life. So even if I refused to help, everyone would've died either way. At least I got away with my soul still intact."

"Blaze, your eyes are missing," I point out. "Why'd he do that?"

"Him?" Blaze asks. "I did that. I couldn't cope with it, so I tore them out. I shoved my fingers behind my eyes and just scooped them from my head."

"Blaze," I whisper. "I'm sorry for what happened. If I was there, maybe I cou-"

"Could what?" Blaze cuts me off. "Die too?"

I pause for a moment, taking a deep breath.

"Look. It's horrible what happened, but you can't see anymore. How is that going to help in any way?" I ask.

"I don't know...I just did it on impulse. I don't think about my actions until after they happen," Blaze tells me. He puts his hands over his face and crouches over. "I'm a mistake. One of the last of my kind, and I can't even save my race."

I open my mouth to speak, but a blinding white light shines upon us as I do. I cover my face with my arms and look up to see a D16-Crack Tiger hovering in the sky. Dangling from the bottom is a man holding onto a tangled white rope, inches above the ground.

"Hey!" the man yells out. He lets go of the rope and drops down onto the ground. He slams against the scorched plains with heavy boots, leaving a deep hole in the dirt. He runs over to us, being slowed down by the heavy gray bodysuit and white helmet he wears.

"Who are you?" I ask, standing up.

"What the fuck happened here?" he asks. "I was just asked by Tyre to go scavenge Roan…and I come back, and it's an inferno?"

I run up to the man, grabbing onto his collar and shaking him back and forth.

"We need to get out of here!" I yell at him. He tries to speak, but a loud rumble of thunder and a blinding flash of red lightning distracts us. We both look past the D16 to a distant black volcano spewing ash from the top in the distance. A circular orange light blasts from the volcano as lava expels out. The light shoots through the air, falling toward us. It lands behind us, next to Blaze, creating a field of smoke.

"What's going on?" Blaze asks, trying to feel around. From the smoke, a white glove reaches out and grabs onto Blaze's neck. He starts choking, trying to scratch at the hand. The grip tightens; veins bulging through the gloves. The fingers then crush through Blaze's next. His head pops off and rolls to the ground, and his body collapses. As the smoke clears, a woman emerges and is illuminated by another strike of orange lighting.

~The Castle~

"You asked to see me, Lord Magona?" Lord Dayag asks, kneeling on the cold gray charred ground. His sunbleached black robes spread across the floor behind him, the ends eternally smoking. He lowers his head, which is covered with a mask of pale green steel, bolted into the skin underneath. Shadows cover the oval eye holes, and the sharp nose casts over the metal bars atop the mouth, akin to stitches. His chapped deep blue mouth is barely visible behind the rods.

"Lord Dayag. As you know, you are my commander in this operation. And as such, I must be the one to inform you of all changes," Magona says from a throne of twisting black vines. His head is covered with a new rust-colored cloak, held together with sheets of black metal across the chest. Both of his arms rest on the armrests of his throne, his fingers tapping against the slimy build. Tubes protruding from his shoulders lead into his sunken cheeks and, through a few holes in his cloak, can be seen wrapping around his chest.
"And I have decided to replace you."

"WHAT?" Lord Dayag calls out. He attempts to stand up but slips on the moist floor, crashing back to the ground.

"You have done such a great job, but…I have since learned of your race," Magona whispers. He removes his hood, and his disturbing face shines in the darkness.
"BRING OUT THE COMMANDER!"

The walls of the ruined Castle Pobomba rumble with the footsteps of Magona's new commander. She walks over the scorched drawbridge and under the entrance archway into the throne room. Standing next to Lord Dayag's fallen body, the commander grabs onto his head and pulls him to his feet. As Lord Dayag is brought up, he gets a good look at her face.

A sharp chin and a slender physique; deep red eyes that bleed through black streaks around the orbital cavities. Fair ivory skin and streaming black hair that flows down to her thighs. Her body is decorated with molten cybernetic plates, seemingly from a salvaged Leathean Machine. High leather black boots reach her knees, and white opera gloves cover her elbows. The only skin showing on her whole body being her face and a small area between her tech-covered shoulder and her gloved forearms.

Her thin, blood-red lips crease into a devious grin as she stares forward at Magona, who claps to her arrival.

"My goodness!" Magona exclaims as he rises from his throne. "You sent shivers down my cracked spine when you walked over that drawbridge!"

"I didn't do anything special, my Lord?" the woman says.

"But you did it better than Lord Dayag could," Magona says. Lord Dayag feels betrayed more than before. Magona steps down from his chair and approaches them. Dayag looks down at the ground as Magona pats the woman's shoulder. "You will do great...Sergeant Airn."

"Thank you, my Lord. What shall we do about this invalid entity?" Airn asks in a wicked voice. Magona's elderly flushed face slightly decays as a smile breaks through his crusty skin.

"Kill," Magona says. A strike of lightning cracks against the ground behind us, and the orange light reflects off Magona's chest piece. Airn drops Dayag to the ground, whose face slams into the coarse dirt; Dayag lifts his head up to see Airn wielding Magona's sword. The orange reflects off the black floor and Dayag's eyes. Airn lowers to her knees and grabs onto Dayag's mask.
She pulls on it, and the metal screws rip skin off Dayag's face. Drops of dark blue blood splash onto the ground as Airn holds the mask in her hand. She throws it to the ground and sets her eyes on Dayag's exposed face.
Light blue skin aged from years of no sunlight and sunken yellow eyes. A mouth of no teeth underneath a crooked, bony nose. Around his face are wounds from the mask's screws, and the deep blue liquids flow across the uneven skin. It's evident that he's an Aqurum, a race mixed between humans and Aquatarsos.

"Humans…the only true race I planned to erase. They just… don't know how to keep themselves off other species. So I made sure to destroy Earth II to prevent more crossbreeding. I can make a new planet with the amount of energy Earth II is down to now. And you thought you could wear that mask to hide the truth?" Magona says.

"My father was a human, yes, but it was consensual with my mother. Most of the time, it's…not," Dayag says.

"Wouldn't that mean I'm a pure race? One made with both parties agreeing?"

"Your pleads are worthless. Nothing changes the fact that you are an inbred monster…product of a species that should have been over with the transfer from Earth I," Magona booms. "Airn, kill him."

Airn nods and throws Magona's sword to her left, the hilt piercing through the stones. Dayag looks at her in confusion as Airn's gloved arms violently vibrate and two shining blood-red daggers quiver into existence. When they solidify, Airn's arms steady, and she grabs onto the black wooden handles. She places the edges of both blades on Dayag's shoulders, and heat courses through his body. He puts his head down, closing his eyes, as he feels the daggers cut through the skin, slicing through his neck and turning his vision black.
Dayag is no more.

"A simple but necessary elimination," Magona scoffs. "Sergeant Airn…as you know, I have a gift."

"It is your sword…the Tophet Sword," Airn responds. "Spare me the lecture, old man."

"You dare to speak to me like that?" Magona booms. A smirk slices through Airn's face, and her red eyes pulse with black electricity.

"I don't give a fuck about your sword…real warriors only need their bare skin and universe-given strength," Airn says back. "You needed to craft a sword to do what you want?"

"Leave my sight," Magona whispers. Airn puts a hand up to her ear, pointing it toward Magona.

"Sorry, I couldn't hear you," she mocks. Magona slams a fist down on his throne, pieces of black vines breaking off and crashing to the ground. He swiftly rises to his knees, storming over to his wall-bound sword. Then, without removing his gaze from Airn, he grabs onto the blade with both hands. Finally, he rips it from the stone and slides the sword beneath his cloak.

"Remove yourself from my sight," Magona says, his voice shaking the walls and Airn's eardrums. She covers her ears and winces in pain as Magona sits back on his throne. "Speak like that to me again, and I will personally make sure Governor Korbrus of Treenun has you put on a Death Cycle."

"You think I'm scared of a little fun?" Airn laughs as she turns her back on Magona and walks back over the drawbridge. Magona watches her travel away, and he pulls out his sword from under his cloak. Finally, he spins it around, examining the fracture where the missing piece should be.

"Where are you?" Magona asks the sword.

"The girl…," a voice whispers back. Magona almost drops the sword from fright.

"Did you…just speak?" he asks the blade. He feels a sensation take over the hand that holds the hilt, one that he can't control. The hand slowly turns the sword down, and Magona loses feeling in his other arm, which is brought forward underneath the lowering blade. "What is happening?"

"She needs to know who you are…," the sword whispers. "You are Magona…the powerful…the mighty…the angelic."

Hearing the word 'angelic' sends Magona into a spiral. The hilt-holding hand suddenly loosens, and the blade drops, sliding through Magona's right arm. At first, nothing is felt, but then sharp pains shoot through his body. His veins bulge, and he screams, holding up his bloody, forearm-less arm.

Magona falls onto the ground, curled up in a fetal position as he cradles his stump, the mangled forearm disintegrating under the sword next to him. The blade slowly lowers as the skin beneath slowly fizzles away. Magona continues to howl as the droplets of dark red blood splash against the black stone floor.

"Grab me…before I fall," the sword echoes. Magona turns over and sees the blade millimeters from touching the ground. He quickly grabs it with his left hand, holding it above his floor-bound body. He holds the hilt against his chest, rolling over onto his back and placing his stubby arm over his cold, sweating forehead.

"Place me…in the wound."

"What?" Magona yells. His milky eyes stare at the sword, feeling the same sensation as before. His left arm steadily leads the blade to Magona's right, the hilt slowly lowering into the open gash of blood and tissue. Magona's deep breathing becomes breaths of pain as the woven handle pulls and tears at the muscle and shredded bone it scrapes against.

The black, viny rain-guard of the Tophet Sword pushes against the edges of skin, and the vines grow and swirl around Magona's arm. The ends wrap around to the top of his right shoulder, where they break through the skin and pierce into Magona's veins. His left hand is then back in his control, and he continues to lay against the moist ground.

The pain is already just another inconvenience; his brain won't even register it anymore. He can only feel the dripping of blood against his skin and the vines writhing around inside. He turns his head to his left, where the corpse of Dayag stares at him with bleeding black eyes and an open mouth. A tear of blood forms in Magona's left eye, but he doesn't care to wipe it away.

"What are you?" Magona asks the blade in his arm, his gaze still directed toward Dayag.

"Your help...," it responds. "Show Gellax you know what you're doing. Think about Earth II...all that energy...why not do it with every planet? You have so many followers...enough to restart life."

"You're right...," Magona says, thinking about it. "These planets will never learn. If they aren't already on my side...they never will."

"Rise, my Lord," the blade says. Magona sits up, and he feels his legs automatically lift his body. He rises to his feet, stumbling for balance at first, and walks to his throne. "You don't need a seat to show anyone who you are…only me can do that."

"Yes…," Magona agrees, slashing at the throne with his sword arm. The black vines let out vibrating screeches, almost like screams, as they wiggle around with each impact of the blade. "Only you…can help me."

Magona begins to laugh, a quiet chuckle at first. As he looks at his orange blade, the chuckle violently grows into maniacal laughter. His head bulges with black veins, and his milky eyes twist into void-black. His bumpy, lipless mouth and disjointed teeth shine as orange lightning crashes around him. He looks up at the sky to see a distant mountain erupting with lava. Magona laughs harder, his voice almost cracking with each rise in volume, as he falls to his knees and watches the black clouds in the sky.

—

Airn opens the disheveled black wooden door to her home. Holes in the wood let through a draft, a cold breeze brushing against Airn's bare upper arms. The door slams shut behind her, and she steps into the cramped, shed-like place she calls her abode. The brown floorboards creak with each step, and black vines wiggle through the gray concrete walls.

Airn steps over to an unbalanced black steel table, taking a seat on a plastic-covered mound of dirt. She removes her gloves, placing them on the table and revealing her bare hands. The skin ends around her elbows, and wrappings of bloodstained white paper with broken pins holding them together cover the muscles until the fingertips. The edges of her fingers are flat; the veins beneath wrapping around her bones and forming into a little red hole at each end.

Airn places the ends of each finger into her mouth and bites down hard. Her jagged white teeth push down on the bundles of veins, and droplets of her own blood drip onto her tongue. She swirls it around her mouth and subtly licks her fingers as they continue to leak. After an entire minute, she loosens the grip, and her fingers cease dripping.

"What are you doing?" someone asks from the darkness behind her. Airn turns to see a silhouette standing in the doorway to her bedroom. The light from beyond the figure shines the back of them, but their wide front is covered in shadow.

"Who are you? And how did you get here?" Airn screams, standing up and backing into the table. The figure waddles closer, and a crash of orange lightning shines through the holes in the door, lighting him up.

A nude, pale, veiny, chubby man, sweating from dandruff-covered head to crusty toe. Flabs of his skin hand off his arms, legs, and stomach like they're trying to jump off his body. Square black glasses sit crooked on his face; one lens cracked, and the other gone completely. An unkempt, black neckbeard stretches down to his purple oval nipples.

As for the hair on his head, it's also black and speckled in little white dots, and it flows down his back and front, down to a pitiful sight. Both his testicles are flattened to his inner thighs, ripped in the middle, and separated by some past event. They're taped and held into his skin by needles, and his shaft is gruesomely stuck to his belly button by some welding practices.

"Listen…please help me," the man says, his voice sticky and dry. He reaches out to Airn, but she quickly sidesteps to the door. "No… don't leave!"

"Who the fuck are you?" Airn screams, quickly grabbing onto her gloves and backing against the broken door. "Get away from me!"

The man hobbles toward Airn with outstretched arms, and Airn howls as she kicks the door down. It crashes against the seared black dirt, and Airn jumps over it. She makes a run toward Magona's castle in the distance, where orange and red lightning crash beyond the silhouetted building. She huffs and struggles for breath as the big man shakes the ground with each step.

Past the mountains, destroyed city houses, and gray skies, Airn passes; over the dirt paths, black vines, and mangled corpses, Airn jumps. To the looming castle of Magona and to freedom, Airn runs; from a Whorm poking its little mushroom-shaped fleshy head, Airn trips. She crashes to the ground, her jaw smashing into her upper lip.

"I've got you now, little lady!" the man yells, catching up to Airn's grounded body. Airn wants to move, but her body won't respond. Instead, she silently watches as the man scoops her body up in his arms, hoisting her over his meaty shoulders. Then, as the man carries Airn away, a mountain nearby erupts with thunderous noise and a flash of orange.

~~

The woman emerges from the smoke.

A blue-skinned Duhv with a bright red three-piece suit, one long bloodstained white glove, and muddy black high heels. She walks like a diva, one leg in front of the other, as a storm begins to brew. Black, tar-like sludge rains from the sky, drenching the three of us; the Duhv, the D16 pilot, and me.

"I don't care for you two. Give me Zarn," she booms. The sludge plops against her bald, bumpy head, sliding past her angled eyes and smirking mouth. "Lanzion, I know you're with him."

"Who's Zarn?" I ask, turning around to see Lanzion holding out a silver double-decker energy blaster. Then, on the tips of both barrels, a small orb of blue energy begins to form.

"I don't have him, Korbrus," Lanzion says back to the Duhv. She growls and leaps onto me, thrashing at my face with sharp pink nails. She lets out a scream, sounding like a mix between a human screech and a gun firing.

"Get her off me!" I yell at Lanzion as her nails slice through my right eye and into my healed skin. Korbrus pulls out some of my hair, ripping it in handfuls. Blood squirts from the wounds onto her face, mixing with the black rain.

"Korbrus, we don't HAVE him…so back off," Lanzion says, stepping over and placing both barrels

162

against Korbrus's bare head. She gently moves away from me as she raises her arms and puts her hands behind her head. "Now, step away and return to Treenun...where you belong."

"I just want Zarn. Give him to me, and I'll let you go," Korbrus pleads. She side-eyes Lanzion as she treads backward, stepping over Blaze's shriveled head.

"Lady, let's go," Lanzion says as he holds out an arm in front of me. I turn to see the rope dangling from the D16 and run for it. My feet kick up dirt as I sprint, the sludge continuing to plunge toward the ground. My soiled, bloodstained fingers wrap around the rough rope, and I hoist myself toward the circular hatch it hangs from, letting out a soft white light.

I reach the top, pushing myself against the floor of the D16 into its front cockpit. Below the narrow window slits that let in the dark orange light from outside is a row of waist-high consoles. Atop the angled console faces, little lights of red and blue blink sporadically, and I can hear faint bloop sounds. Two cushioned stationary chairs sit before them; one is empty while the other is occupied.

"Hello?" the sitter asks in a deep voice, sounding very forced. He spins around to face me, and a puffy brown perm shines from a strike of lightning outside. His sharp, well-defined pale yellow face and chiseled chest reflect the dim white light above me. On his legs, comfortable gray pants flow as if caught in a breeze, despite the lack of such.

"Zarn?" I ask. He nods.

"Janx. Welcome aboard!" a robotic yet human voice cheers from behind me. I turn to see a scraggly, bare, light blue android step through the sliding cabin door. On each joint, a broad line separates each part, and scrappy rags cover the exposed wiring. His vivid yellow eyes and abnormally tall forehead distract from the hanging blue dong between his legs.

"Yeah, yeah, yeah, cut the chatter and let's get out of here," Lanzion says, climbing up the hatch. It closes behind him, and he slides past me, sitting on the empty chair. He presses some buttons on the console, and the narrow windows open wider, showing off a higher view of Loca.

For all I can see, the scorched black ground of Loca equals the darkness of the clouds. The only light outside is from the occasional lightning strike, the erupting volcano far behind us, and the pink sun trying its best to shine upon the soil.

"You two, get out," Lanzion says, shooing the android and me out. We both walk out of the cockpit, me first and then the robot behind me. Then, we enter the main chamber, where rows of light blue and white beds line the shining silver walls. Bright yellow light shines down, and on the far wall, a glass box holds some sort of creature within.

"How do you know my name?" I quickly ask as soon as I hear the slam of the cabin door.

"My name is 8088-Y, a Leathean Machine. One of the model-C8e variety," the android responds.

"Row-N?" I ask, thinking about the last time I saw him and one of his machines. "You look so…different than the rest."

8088-Y laughs, covering his stomach with his hands and leaning back as he does.

"Well, he's had quite a while to perfect his work since your unfortunate…disappearance," he says. I'm reminded of the fact that I was gone for so long to them, but a matter of hours to me. For so long that Row-N was able to make a near-perfect specimen; for so long that Loca was overtaken by death and darkness.

"How did you all find me?" I ask. 8088-Y smiles.

"Well, Row-N made ME specifically to find you, and he implanted a chip within you. I was alerted of your location when you got to a certain distance above the core. So I had to beg the crew to rush over here, and I'm glad I did," he explains. "Please, you need to lay down."

He motions over to the row of beds, to which I choose the very middle one. I pat down on the bouncy mattress, wiping off some crumbs from under the fluffy white pillow. Climbing onto the bed, I lay my head down and close my eyes. The ringing in my ears cease, and the thoughts in my head come together and form a simple dream.

—

The quiet hum of the D16 engines is the first thing I hear when I awake. My eyes take a moment to focus, and I look up at 8088-Y, the green body encased in the glass behind him.

"What…who…is that?" I ask, pointing at it. 8088-Y turns to it for a moment, then looks back at me.

"That is someone we picked up from a scavenge on Roan," he responds. I inch back in shock.

"Roan is still around? I thought it was destroyed."

"Well, the social tower, climate, population, and the Province of Maxxersh were…but the asylum and purple seas still remain," 8088-Y says. The discussion is halted as the cabin door slams open. Lanzion storms out while still in a conversation with Zarn.

"…and just know, she's going to come back, and you can't pussy out again. Fucking worthless," Lanzion yells. When the door closes, he turns to us and lets out a deep breath. "Apologies, both of you. So! You must be Janx."

"Yes," I respond. Lanzion walks over and pats both of my shoulders, swiping some dirt off the jacket. He smiles, his pastel green cheeks swirling into a light red. I notice some sort of dot in the middle of his forehead, slightly covered by a strand of pink hair. Then, as I squint my eyes for a better look, the hole closes, and the skin evens out.

"I've heard a lot about you. Shame about Row-N and Reez," he says.

"What happened to Row-N?" I frighteningly ask. Lanzion turns his head to 8088-Y.

"Didn't tell her?" he asks.

"How could I? She could've lived without the truth," 8088-Y responds. I quickly slide myself off the bed;

onto my bare heels. Then, I grab the collar of Lanzion's gray bodysuit, shaking him about. "Lanzion, tell her."

"Where are they?" I yell. Lanzion gulps and looks into my eyes.

"They were probably killed by Magona. Almost everyone on Loca was," Lanzion explains. "When we heard the news on our way here, I almost backed out. But 8088-Y insisted we find you."

"Why?" I ask, turning to 8088-Y. "Why did Row-N need to find me?"

"Because Reez told him everything, and through Row-N, told me everything," 8088-Y says. "Janx, you're...not human."

"Well, obviously," I say, letting go of Lanzion's collar. "I'm sub-human; mostly comprised of Astral DNA."

"That is exactly it," 8088-Y says. He walks over to the glass cage, standing in front of a tiny keypad on the wall next to it. He presses a few little gray buttons until the ceiling opens, and a claw emerges. It's holding a silver and white mallet, which it smashes the glass with.

"Who is that?" I ask.

"Janx, you are one of seven souls with demi-Astral DNA," 8088-Y responds. "Reez and Tyre had it as well, and I observed some in that man you were with behind the dirt mound on Loca."

The glass continues to shatter as the hammer bashes through the thick material. Inside, the green creature breathes through its peach skin, covered by the molding husk. A jar beside him throbs with blue light, and a jagged wooden staff pulses with unseen energy.

"This man, creature, whatever he is, is made of one-hundred-percent demi-Astral DNA," 8088-Y says. "Which makes you part of him."

"What?" I yell out; at that exact moment, the cage fractures and falls to the ground. The green man crashes to the floor, the whole ship almost flipping due to his weight. The staff clinks on the steel ground next to him, and the jar also falls.

"Janx, you are a demiGod," 8088-Y finally answers. "And this...is The Seventh God."

"Where...am I?" The Seventh cries out. "I... can't see... can't feel...anything."

I run over to him, rolling him onto his back and holding him up with my arms. His cracking green face shell looks up in my direction with milky black eyes. I slip a finger through a hole in the husk, wiping against his slimy peach skin.

"Energy...why is it warm?" The Seventh asks. He feels around my jacket, patting it down until his hand lands atop the shard pocket. "It's...no. Get this off the ship."

"What?" I ask. Lanzion runs over and grabs the back of my jacket, attempting to pull it off. I try to resist, but his grip is too firm, and he tears it from my back. He stumbles back from the force, and I turn to see him crumbling it up into a ball.

"Give me back that jacket," I demand.

"No…the energy is of Magona…and that's the last trace of him," The Seventh says. "Rid of it, now."

"Lanzion, don't you fucking dare," I yell at him, but I am met with ignorance. Lanzion walks into the cabin with the jacket, and I drop The Seventh's head onto the ground as I crawl onto my feet. Bolting to the door, 8088-Y steps in my way, but I push him aside with my shoulder. He crashes into the ship's side, knocking over a few of the beds.

I pound on the cockpit door, demanding to be let in, but I'm only met with silence.

"LET ME IN! THROW THE FUCKING SHARD AWAY; JUST GIVE ME BACK THAT JACKET!"

"Janx, please," 8088-Y tries to say from the ground.

"I want you to keep your fucking mouth shut," I yell through flowing tears. I lean my head on the door as I sniffle, my bare shoulders longing for the jacket's warmth. I wrap my arms around my goosebump-ridden chest, slowly lowering myself to the ground. "Reez…I miss you."

~The Al-X~

Airn sniffs the stale, bitter air. A trickle of blood flows out one of her dirty nostrils. She breathes heavily, making sure to savor every taste of the air. She sits on a taped-up metal folding chair, bound to it by a few tight loops of itchy tan rope. Across her gloved arms and plated chest are abundant cuts, blood staining the area around them.

In front of her, the overweight man stands formally before a circular window that displays the nighttime Province of Carishem. The only lights are from the houses and storefronts outside, illuminating the otherwise dark room Airn finds herself in.

"Who are you?" Airn asks. She wiggles her fingers, attempting to slip them out of the binds. The man stares out the window, looking out to a bright neon tower. It flashes with advertisements and images that are usually bundled together with casinos. The building towers over all around it; a large shadow being cast over the town.

"I used to be powerful," he says, almost sorrowfully. "A man…sitting on his throne. What happened? How did it come to this?"

"You're…Al-X?" Airn asks, in complete shock. "Everyone thought you were dead."

Al-X turns around, and his angered face is drowned in darkness, and luckily, so is his battered crotch. A strike of lightning outside crashes into a random house; a blast of orange and red light booms into the air.

"I was underground, trying to catch a little bitch that ran from me. All of the entrances were cut off...and I had to stay in a temple for who knows how long," Al-X explains. "I was finally freed when someone else found a staircase to the surface. I was out...and didn't care to wait for the other survivor."

"Why did you take me? And why are you still here?" Airn cries out, and Al-X has a hearty laugh, sounding very sarcastic.

"I had one business that prospered throughout my time here, and it was my auctions," Al-X says. He turns back to the window and looks out into the gray skies. "I would always keep one for myself...but I would have to kill them for the next one."

"Keep...what?" Airn fearfully asks.

"A woman."

Unbeknownst to Airn, a smile creeps through Al-X's brittle lips. He places a hand onto the glass, right over the view of the casino. Airn wiggles around, trying to knock the chair over, but it remains in place. She tries to push against the ground with her feet, but the bottom of her boots are too smooth and slip against the concrete floor.

"And so we'll both stay here...forever...and you will bear all the children I want," Al-X cheers. A crack forms when he pushes on the glass where his hand is. He applies more pressure, and the window begins to shatter, the shards crashing to the ground and around Al-X's bare feet. "And maybe father will come...to help you or to finally raise me."

"Father?" Airn asks, stopping her escape.

"Magona...my maker," Al-X answers. "I need him...to see how much I've evolved!"

—

Magona walks across the burnt plains of Loca, his wrinkly pale bare feet smoldering on the bottom. He drags the sword behind him, the broken tips inches above the ground. In this middle of nowhere, a heavily scorched patch of grass lies underneath a bundle of cloth. Magona steps before the object, kneeling down and grabbing onto it.

He stands back up, letting the fabric unwrap into a neat leather jacket. As it unfolds, a small shining piece of glass falls onto the ground. Magona's eyes quickly shift down, seeing an orange glow emitting from the shard. He feels a connection to the object and the whispers from his sword.

"There...grab it...make me whole," the sword says. Magona points his bladed arm at the final piece, and it suddenly shoots up and connects to the blade. Then, a burst of energy blasts out, blazing all of the land around. His face twitches, and his eyelids frantically open and close; his veins bulge, his skin shrinks until the muscles pop, and all that's left is bone.

Magona jerks from his trance, plummeting onto the ground, his sword nearly tapping a blade of black grass. He stares into the orange light, seeing his reflection, skin warping around the bone, his own skull peeking through tears on his forehead. His milky eyes are now black; voids that stare back at him. A shaky, trembling mouth above a shredded chin. As he closes his eyes, the sword speaks once more.

"And maybe father will come…," it says, in a different, more congested voice. "To finally raise me."

"Al-X…," Magona quietly lets out. "I will accept you as my kin. Just tell me where you are."

Another blast of orange emerges from his blade, sweeping through the land but not burning it this time. Magona fully closes his eyes, letting his brain connect to one growing in Carishem.

—

"Evolved? In what way?" Airn asks.

"Well."

As Al-X prepares to answer, a field of orange light enters the room through the broken window, covering Al-X but fading inches before Airn's bound body.

"What was that?" she asks. Al-X doesn't answer. Instead, he places his grubby hands on his moldy hair. "Hello?"

"There's something under my skin," Al-X says. "It's wriggling around, and I don't like it."

"Excuse me?" Airn replies. Al-X swiftly rotates, pulling down on his hair, clumps falling out and blood pooling from the rips. He continues to drag his fingers across his face, the long, uncut fingernails slicing through his forehead. They slide through his eyes, the orbs popping with red and clear liquids.

"I DON'T WANT TO FEEL LIKE THIS," Al-X screams. "THE SKIN HURTS TO WEAR."

Al-X's hands bulge with veins as he pushes his nails deeper, pulling the skin off his cheeks. It exposes the muscles underneath, which pulse with movements. Spongy pink material leaks out from his gaping mouth, dripping down his dry lips. He tears his fingers from his face, blood, and pieces of skin flying across the room as he does so. A few drops land on Airn's face, who tries to get them off by shaking her head around.

"TEAR IT OFF, TEAR IT OFF," Al-X continues to scream, his voice muffling from his filling mouth. He latches onto his shoulders, and Airn closes her eyes and turns her head away as Al-X pulls the rest of his skin off. After what seems like an eternity of muffled screams and moans from Al-X, the sounds stop with the boom of a thud on the ground.

Airn shakingly opens her eyes, looking upon the mangled corpse of Al-X; his muscles' pink and red colors, along with the pile of bloodstained skin he rests upon. The back of his head leans up on a baseboard lining the walls, staring at Airn. A black-eyed skull, with lumps of hair and skin, still overtop, leaking from all open gaps with a pink sludge.

"My son...," Airn hears Magona say from behind her. "What have you done?"

"Magona, my Lord, please let me out," Airn pleads. Magona walks into view, trembling at the sight of Al-X. He kneels next to the corpse, creeping his fingers into the open mouth. He slowly thrusts his arm into Al-X's throat, grabbing onto as much pink as possible.

"To think…I could remake his brain," Magona cries out. "Bring his connection back."

"My Lord, what happened?" Airn asks. Magona swiftly turns his head toward her.

"You shut your mouth and sit there, you hag," Magona screams at Airn. He redirects his attention to Al-X, where he pulls his arm back out, his hand moist with the goo from the pink muck. He slowly closes his eyes, placing the goo into his mouth. He leisurely chews it, the sploshing sounds echoing through my ears.

He eats it with his mouth open, and gloops of milky liquid splash out of his lips. He suggestively moans as he consumes what Airn thinks is now a brain. Magona finally swallows the lot, sexually groaning as he does. He licks his nonexistent lips, licking the slimy slush off his face.

"WHAT THE FUCK," Airn screams out.

"I grew that brain…and now it cannot go to waste," Magona says. "All of the memories, feelings, and everything that he felt. I must retain it all."

He continues to remove more brain, chewing each handful with erotic movements and sounds. Magona scurries and climbs atop Al-X's corpse, shoving his mouth into the gaping throat of Al-X.

"Sergeant Airn...we have a change of plans,"
Magona says through violent chews. "I have fused with the
sword and can hear its thoughts. It wants me to kill all life
that doesn't already follow me. If it's not part of my
religious order by now, it never will be."

"Please just get me out of here...I want to go
home," Airn pleads through tears of horror. She tries to
wiggle out, but the rope remains tight. Magona whirls his
head around as Airn says, 'home.' He snarls like a rabid
animal, drool pooling at the corners of his starved lips, and
his eyes appear black and nonexistent.

"Your home will be the first to go," he says, his
voice deep and demonic. "I will send all of my people to
the remains of Roan. From there, we shall transfigure all of
these planets into the necessary energy to start anew.
These worlds have already been touched by false-races'
slimy hands."

"My Lord, I just want to leave," Airn cries.

"I will have to kill you if you wish to disband my
group," Magona says, turning back to the corpse. "Besides,
I know you live with adopted parents. I killed your real
ones at the beginning of my quest; you really are an old
woman."

"They were among your first followers...and I was
born right after your disappearance, my Lord," Airn says.
"Please, I-I can do so much for you. I KILLED DAYAG,
FOR FUCKS SAKE."

Magona shakes a wrinkled, bony finger toward
Airn. He arches up and stumbles forward with his knees

bent inward. Each step rumbles through his skin, and his black eyes swirl to reveal two milky yellow orbs with a black slit down the middle of both. His gaunt face puffs with strings of muscle growing underneath the skin. Black vines wrap around his right arm, latching onto the bottom of the blade and holding it in place.

"Just because you spilled blood doesn't make you special," he says. "I just wanted you to…feel special, perhaps."

"Let me go back to my family, and I can support you from afar," Airn pleads. The words cause Magona to laugh, his dry mouth cracking and dust falling from the tongue. Airn squints her eyes and turns her head in fear and horror as Magona steps closer.

"You have two choices," Magona says. "Return to your…guardians…and perish with the rest of the planet. Or you can continue being my sergeant. Which will it be?"

—

"SOMEONE, PLEASE! HELP ME!" Tyre screams as he shakingly pulls himself across the temple floor. His fractured spine drags along behind him; blood smeared along the ground. His dark skin is dotted with heavy beads of sweat, and his neon green eyes water with painful tears.

All through his body, he can feel nothing but pain. He's already removed the tight black bodysuit he wore; it confiscated his ability to breathe after being split. His fingernails crack and bleed from the force Tyre crawls along with. Strands of white hair hang over his face, blocking part of his view.

Tyre's bloodcurdling screams for help echo through the endless hall. He's met with only the silence of the books and the constant ringing of pain in his ears. Eventually, he gives up trying to survive and lowers his head onto the ground. He can't even feel the coldness of the stones below.

"Don't give up on me," someone says from above him. Tyre uses the last of his strength to lift his head back up. He's met with the view of a towering figure of fire. A slender yet built shape made from the gas of the Infinite Flames; a section of negative energy lightyears away that can create sentient, forever burning beings.

"Who...are you?" Tyre stutters out.

"I am Avix," she responds. Avix bends her knees and grabs Tyre's bruised shoulders. "Aw...look at you. All battered and beaten up."

"What are you?"

Tyre expects the flames of Avix to burn, but he feels no heat. Avix slides her hands onto Tyre's neck, bringing his upper half to her eight-foot height. Tyre tries to support his own head, but the weight is too much, and it lowers.

"What did I tell you?" Avix says. Tyre tries again to stay awake, moving only his eyes to see Avix's glowing face. Inside the border of flames, two black orbs hovering before a slushy purple brain. "Maybe if I form as someone you want to kill?"

The appearance of Avix burns brighter as her waist thins more, and the shape of breasts form on her chest. She even grows a few more inches in height, adding to her already tall stature. Her 'smooth' blazing head creates thin strands of flames that act as long, straight hair.

"How do you know...about Janx?" Tyre asks.

"Silly Tyre," she says. Tyre's eyes slowly close as he falls unconscious from the blood loss. "You need to be strong. Reach for your hatred for Janx and-"

"Enough," a voice booms from the darkness. Avix drops Tyre's body onto the ground, turning to see a bumbling amalgamation of dark metal plates held together with bloodstained teal ropes. A head of eight cracked orbs illuminates the area in front of the android. "He's in enough pain."

"Row, you're the one that wanted him to suffer," Avix responds. The robot stands over Tyre's body and grabs a handful of his hair. He lifts him up, holding onto snow-white strands as they begin to tear from his scalp. Tyre quickly awakens and shoots his arms up, grabbing onto the androids.

"GET OFF ME! LET ME DIE!" Tyre yells, his voice shattered and crushed. He sets his green eyes on the robot, instantly recognizing the craft of the build. "Row-N? I was looking all OVER for you! Everyone thought you died."

"Looking for ME?" Row-N's voice booms. "I decided to go into Carishem because you kidnapped Janx and flew to Al-X's casino like you owned the place. Then, Janx was GONE, you were GONE, and I was the one

FOUND. Tortured…for how long? Apparently not enough to kill me."

"Row, I can explain. I thought we could use Juwles' parasitic sludge to kill Al-X!" Tyre pleads. The strands of hair continue to rip, a few popping from his head.

"And where did that lead?" Row-N asks. "Juwles even said it wasn't ready. And since that singular mistake YOU made led to all of this happening, we decided that you should fix it."

"What are you going to do? Infect me with that? I used the last dose," Tyre laughs.

"We're making sure that was the last mistake you ever make," Row-N says. He nods at Avix, who disappears into the flaming darkness. Tyre waits for a moment, and when Avix re-emerges, she carries a steel cage with both hands. Behind bars, a dark creature writhes around.

"What's that?" Tyre asks in fear.

"Something you didn't even know existed," Row-N laughs. He lets go of Tyre's hair, and he crashes onto the ground, cracking his jaw. He looks up as Avix turns the cage's door toward him, and she slides the gate open. A wobbly oil-black flesh creature stumbles on two flabby legs, an umbilical cord dragging along the ground behind it.

"WHAT IS THAT?" Tyre screams out as the gaping mouth of the creature grabs onto his nose, sharp fangs growing from the gums and slicing through Tyre's skin. Tyre lets out a bloodcurdling scream as the child backs its head away, bringing Tyre's nose with it. Blood squirts across the floor, and the nose drops onto the mess. Tyre opens his mouth as much as he can to howl in terror as the baby drops onto its stomach and pushes itself forward with its legs.

The fetus sticks its bubbly head into Tyre's open mouth, to which he tries to blow it out. The baby isn't phased and continues to squirm into Tyre's throat. Avix looks away and covers her mouth, but Row-N continues to watch the violence.

Tyre's neck swells up as the creature drags itself down into his digestive tract. Then, Tyre's head crashes against the stones as the baby reaches the middle stomach. Row-N finally looks away as the rectum tube straightens and sticks out underneath the exposed spine. The bell-shaped end of the track expands as the child slides out, covered in feces and sludgy green acid. Finally, it lets out a high-pitched laugh and continues to glide around the floor.

"It's done," Row-N finally says. Avix returns and retches; brown liquid with chunks of green and yellow sliding through her fingers. "How can you do that?"

"I borrowed someone's stomach," Avix responds through a mouth full of vomit. She lowers her arms to reveal a digestive tract floating around her flaming stomach. "I'm getting rid of this."

"May you rest in the darkness of Death's shadow," Row-N says. "Old friend."

As Row-N and Avix walk into the darkness to the Mushrumain cave's entrance, Death fizzles into the area.

His hunched-back appearance and yellow-aged bones match the greasy brown rags he wears. Death kneels and places a bony hand on Tyre's bare back.

"Four of seven…," Death says. "Dead."

Death takes his hand and reaches for his hood, where a small makeshift pocket holds a small folded piece of brown parchment. On the paper, a list reads:

-The Lover

-~~The Soldier~~ DEAD

-The Hypocrite

-~~The Misguided~~ DEAD

-The Watcher

-~~The Follower~~ DEAD

-The Shadow

He writes 'Dead' next to 'The Hypocrite' and crosses the name out, watching as Tyre's body fades into Death's realm. Death feels a soft coldness on his shoulder and turns to see a white ghostly apparition of The Star, a body with a four-pointed face.

"Another part of him?" The Star asks. Death nods.

"Only three left. I know The Lover can survive; she already has made it this far," Death explains. "The Watcher can hold his own, but he's not going to make it out alive. As for The Shadow…."

"No hope?" The Star asks.

"Do you blame me?" Death asks back. "For all I know, The Shadow could be part of Magona's army. He definitely represents the Magona part of The Seventh."

"Will The Seventh save everything?" The Star thinks aloud.

"No," Death responds. "If anything, he'll get to the very end, and something will change his mind."

"Let's hope it's something good," The Star says. He disappears, and Death folds the paper back up and places it in his hood pocket. He stands and fades out of existence, returning to his realm.

—

Avix stands above Blaze's decapitated corpse, admiring her old lover. She scoops some dirt up, placing it on his body.

"What are you doing?" Row-N asks as he scouts the surrounding area. Avix smooths out the dirt grave and places a few random stones around it.

"We used to date a while ago," she responds. "Just a few one-night stands, nothing special."

"My ally, Juwles, helped him for a moment in a medical center underground," Row-N says. "Right before he was used to burn it all down."

"He WHAT?" Avix screams out.

"Calm down," Row-N says, holding out a hand. "He was made to do it. Threatened with his life…and I bet he regretted it after."

"He died in vain?" Avix asks, placing one final circular gray stone atop where Blaze's head is buried. "At least he lived a fiery life. Ha."

Row-N lets out a light chuckle at the pun. He smiles and continues to look in the distance at the mountains and orange lightning that burn at the Loca dirt. He catches the movement of a speedy creature rushing through the wind. Row-N's two large red eyes spin around; his little body inside the head watches upon a screen as the eyes magnify his view.

He sees the being's dark gray trench coat flutter in the wind before a flash of neon shatters Row-N's screen. The robot puts its fist up in defense, and the enemy blurs across the ground. As he slides past Row-N, he slows down, and Avix turns to see the person.

A five-armed, pale-skinned being of unknown race; yellow and orange patterns of stars and moons lining the coat reaching his ankles. Each of his five hands dons black leather fingerless gloves, and each holds onto a crystal white double-neck guitar adorned with bright flashing lights.

The guitar's body is embellished with yellow and green neon circles, and the frame is a clean-cut rectangle. Attached to either side of the body are two Darthros teeth; off-white seventeen-inch fangs from the mouth of a predatory Darthros. The ends of these teeth are adorned with the stained neon green blood of a mysterious death.

The man stomps one of his feet into the ground, and his blurry body snaps into clarity. He hangs his head low, unwashed black hair hanging in clumps over his face. His heavy breaths create puffs of fog, despite the warmth of the air. He turns to Avix, and she sees the rest of his outfit.

A dark blue and red striped shirt with a torn collar, overlapping wrinkled light gray pants. Around his lengthy, muscular neck is a pair of listening devices; two cushiony black ear covers held together with a bendable stem. He lowers his guitar and sticks the teeth into the dirt, and when he lets go, it stands up by itself.

"Hello, sir," he says. "Nice to meet you."

"I don't think I got your name," Row-N says, looking in a random direction. "Nor can I see you."

The man wipes his hair from his face, and a giant pink burn across his left eye is uncovered. His large, sparkling green eyes squint as his thin, lipless mouth smirk. A little white fang hangs from his mouth, shining in the orange light.

"Avix, it has been a million fortnights since I last saw you," the man says. He holds up one of Avix's flaming hands and lays a small kiss on it. Avix blushes; her face brightens as it continues to burn hotter. "And yet, you are still as alluring as you were when we first met."

"Zhalk...you should knock before following me," Avix responds. Zhalk lets go of her hand and retreats to behind the guitar.

"Listen, I know we ended on bad terms...and it seems you have a new man," Zhalk says. Avix rolls her black orbs around in her head.

"Zhalk, I was hired by Row-N here to assist him in some clean-up," Avix explains. "And nowhere did he mention you would show up."

"Ok, ok," Zhalk says as he puts his hands up and backs away. "I did come here for a reason, and specifically to you. You both need to get off Loca."

"Yeah, we know. We're busy trying to finish our business," Row-N says. Zhalk steps in front of Row-N and wipes all eight of his eyes off. Row-N's inside screen flips back on, and he sees the face of Zhalk mouth 'sorry.'

"No, I mean NOW," Zhalk says. "Not far from here, there's some sort of hole in the ground near Carishem. All sorts of shits coming out of it."

"What?" Row-N exclaims. "Could it be from the hole Al-X made? He drilled down to the temple right after Janx went missing…."

"The girl that Tyre kidnapped?" Avix asks. "That's who you're talking about?"

"Same one, yeah," Row-N responds. "Zhalk, what does the hole look like? And is it near the middle of the town?"

Zhalk nods his head as his eyebrows raise.

"It's almost like the pit is filling with lava. This orange light is just illuminating the area around it, and all these like…black vines are wiggling out of it at an alarming rate," Zhalk explains. "You can see it all the way from Beriackhayv."

"What are you doing in the Fivtie ring?" Avix asks. She storms over to Zhalk and looks him dead in the eyes. Zhalk crouches down and tries to hide behind his guitar.

"I was visiting Queen Mholie when the light shone past the planet," Zhalk quickly responds. "I knew you lived here, so I came down to check what was going on, and that's when I discovered all of this wack shit happening."

"Avix, it's Magona," Row-N cuts in. "I bet you the temple is-"

Row-N is interrupted as the sound of wood smashing against itself echoes around them. They all turn to the mound of dirt hiding a temple entrance, seeing a purple light glowing from behind it. Avix slowly approaches the mound, and a glowing woman appears from around the corner, running past Avix.

"WOAH! HEY!" Row-N yells, running after the fleeing woman. Lavender crystals growing from her pale, smooth skin light up the darkness around her as she runs. Zhalk jumps up and grabs onto his guitar, closing one eye and pointing the sharp tooth end of the body at the woman in the distance. He steps a little to the left so that Row-N isn't in the middle of his view.

Zhalk holds the guitar behind him for a moment, then launches his arm forward. He lets go of the double-necks, and the guitar spins through the brittle air until the head smashes into the back of the woman's. A few crystal shards crack off, and she trips on air and falls onto the ground. Row-N tries to skin to a halt by putting his feet forward but ends up sliding forward and slamming onto the dirt.

The guitar lands next to the woman's cracked skull; the cords torn out and slowly squirming in the wind. Avix reaches the fallen girl, holding her up in her arms. The woman's round face drips with mud and dark purple blood, which match her mauve eyes. Avix places a hand on the girl's smooth forehead, feeling the coldness of the touch.

"The temple...," the woman speaks through harsh breaths. "It's crumbling."

"Who is she?" Zhalk asks as he struggles to lift Row-N's solid machine body. Row-N pushes him aside and easily sits up by himself. Zhalk stumbles back and walks around Row-N to crouch next to Avix.

"Please tell me Janx is alive," the woman says. Avix looks at Row-N, who stares at the ground.

"We don't know," he answers. The woman whimpers as a streak of purple blood flow from both thin nostrils. Her face scrunches up as solid, crystalized clear tears form in her closed eyes.

"It's most likely possible!" Row-N says. He pushes himself onto his feet, marching over and looking at the woman's face.

"We need to leave, Zhalk," Avix yells out. She continues to hold the woman in her fiery yet cold arms as Zhalk rushes up and shoves a hand into his coat. He scrounges around for a moment until he pulls out a small, chipped red box.

"I'll call my captain," he says, putting the box up to his mouth and pushing down on a black side button with his thumb. A crash of yellow lightning flashes behind him. "You still have my tracking beacon? Get here, NOW."

"How long until he arrives?" Avix asks. Zhalk shrugs his shoulders and scratches his messy black hair. "Ok, Row-N, you need to assist with her."

"You got it," Row-N says. He squats down and slides his arms under the woman's back, raising her onto his shoulder. The woman continues to weep as Avix approaches Zhalk.

"Thank you for coming…," she whispers. Zhalk places one of his five hands on her transparent flaming cheek. "We can discuss this on the ship."

"I'll tell you everything I've gotten up to," Zhalk laughs. Avix lets out a chuckle to it as well. "Also, you are really easy to find. Especially since you stand out on this black and gray planet."

With the end of his sentence, the mechanical buzzing of a C15-Tranz Hopper silences the whirling of the winds. The black, rectangular body of the craft breaks through the dark clouds, two white spotlights on the bottom shining upon the group. Pieces of metal plates hang off the sides; exposed wiring sparking as the rusty, disarranged ship lowers to the ground.

Six poles lower from holes on the bottom of the C15, and they support the ship as it rests upon the dirt. Steam blasts from tubes that wrap around the body, and the ship rocks as it lands. Zhalk walks to the side of the C15 and knocks on an inapposite neon green panel with his knuckles. The plate is pulled off on the other side, and the inside yellow light shines upon Zhalk's face.

A face appears in the hole, silhouetted from the back. He looks at Zhalk for a moment, then nods, placing the green plate back in place. Zhalk turns back to the others and motions for them to join. Row-N holds onto the woman's back as he and Avix walk up to the C15. A lofty metal panel on Zhalk's left slides away, and an entrance is made.

Zhalk climbs into the ship, staying crouched to help as Row-N slides the woman off his shoulders. He holds onto her arms as Zhalk grabs her legs, pulling her onto the C15's floor. She's dragged away by the captain as Row-N stumbles his way onto the ship. Avix is next, but her height aids her as she quickly lifts one leg up and mounts the craft. Behind her, the door slides closed with a resounding thud.

"Is there any sort of medical supplies on this ship?" Row-N asks. "I excel in medicine and healing."

"Yeah, I think in there," Zhalk says, pointing to a doorframe opposite the cabin entrance. "I think that's where the captain stored that girl."

"Ok, you better have what I need to fix her cracked skull," Row-N says, storming off through the grimy, matte silver interior and under the flickering yellow lights. Avix slides her hands against the blank walls, wiping grease from them. The captain walks out from the other room, quickly passing by Zhalk and entering through the cockpit door before anyone can see him.

"Don't mind him; he's not social," Zhalk says.

"You came to check on me?" Avix cuts him off. "Or were you reminded of me when you went to Carishem?"

"I would tell you to take a seat, but," Zhalk begins. "There's legit nothing in here. Where is all the furniture?"

"Answer me, please," Avix says, looking into Zhalk's eyes. Zhalk hesitates for a moment, gulping before responding.

"Listen, I...always think about you. A lot," Zhalk says. "And honestly, if that beam of light wasn't from Loca, I wouldn't have checked it out. I would've seen where it came from, then turned around. It's not of my business. But it was from Loca, and I wanted to ensure you weren't in danger."

"Zhalk...," Avix says. "You have no idea what you got in the middle of. Loca isn't the same anymore. So I had to spend years dodging search parties and the threat of Magona."

"Who?" Zhalk asks. "What are you talking about?"

"You don't know who Magona is?" Avix asks in complete surprise. "He's slaughtered three planets worth of beings. Wait...how long have you been in the Fivtie ring for?"

"About like...seven to eight rotations of Beriackhayv around the Crieyath Sun," Zhalk responds. "It IS a Cosmo-Edge ring, Avix."

"I know," Avix says, hitting her forehead against the murky wall. "Fuck, you all don't even know what's going on in the Mesial ring. Listen, Zhalk. I don't know what we're going to do. We are very, VERY screwed."

"Magona is that bad, huh?" Zhalk laughs.

"Zhalk, this isn't a laughing matter!" Avix yells out, turning to face Zhalk. "He WILL kill you and Row-N, and who knows, maybe even the captain."

"What about you?" Zhalk asks. "Why not you?"

"He kills false-races, Zhalk," Avix responds. She backs into the wall and slides down onto her knees. Her eyes impossibly water as she places a hand over her mouth. "I was made when the universe was. You and Row-N are both cross-breed species."

"Fuck," Zhalk says. The sudden shock and roar of the engine shake the ship as Zhalk shoots his head toward the cabin door. He walks over, and it opens, allowing him to walk through. Then, entering the cabin, Zhalk sits on a cushioned chair next to the captain, who clicks away at a console of blinking red lights.

Zhalk looks through the window slits to see the scorched land of Loca. Strikes of orange lightning continue to crash in the distance, and the outside smell of burning slithers into the ship. Zhalk loudly sighs as he sits back in the bending chair, placing a hand over his sweating forehead.

"How'd it go with the lady?" the captain asks, his voice sounding feminine. Zhalk laughs in pain as he sits back up. "Tell her you still love her yet?"

"She obviously knows… I'm not subtle," Zhalk responds. He laughs again, albeit a very fake one. The captain turns around, and his appearance surprises Zhalk. "Queen Mholie?"

"Yes!" she yells out. Her dirty blonde hair and dimpled light green face suit the heavenly soft white crystal dress she wears. Her mint skin radiates in the bright yellow cockpit light, similar to the shine on Zhalk's left eye burns.

"Why are you piloting my ship? I told you to stay behind," Zhalk says. Mholie laughs.

"Your captain was busy in the lavatory, so I decided to give it a shot," she says. Zhalk groans as he lays back in his chair. "Where to?"

"Just…get us off Loca," Zhalk responds. "Back to a happier area."

—

In the quiet, peaceful village of Sypoko, a rumble through the ground disturbs the small fishing town near the coast of the Eastern Inaz Stretch. The residents poke their heads out of their compact wooden houses, searching for the quake's source.

"An erfcake?" an elderly, white-haired Felishe asks as he rakes some fallen brown leaves. He uses the metal rake for balance as he straightens his hunched back. Finally, he looks over the Great Sypoko Lake toward the pink snow-topped mountains of Gnusmug. "Whafs going on?"

The calming smoothness of the blue river is eradicated as an orange light shines below. Cracks of yellow and red lightning blast from the water, waves rushing toward land. The lightning erupts into the clouds, turning the white fluffs into dark gray shadows. Magona rises from the water, his blade held high and his wrinkly body dripping with blue.

"My dear residents of Inaz, it is now your time to be used as fuel for a new life," Magona says, his voice being carried throughout the planet. Everyone hears him, and they all scream and panic as Magona begins to walk across the river. His feet glide across the water, dragging his blade through it. The blue stream bleeds with red, large eyes forming through the ground deep below. From Inaz's bordering planets, the residents watch up above as the green and beige Inaz surface is slowly flooded with black and orange.

Loca was first, and now Inaz is suffering the same fate.

~The Station~

"Miss Janx, do you wish for any sort of edibles?" 8088-Y asks, sitting next to me. I'm curled against the cabin door, which hasn't been opened since Lanzion went in with my jacket.

"No thanks," I respond, hiding my head behind my knees.

"Very well. I'll be assisting The Seventh in the other room," 8088-Y says. He stands himself up and walks to where the glass cage was before, a door akin to the cockpit one in its place. The door slides open, and 8088-Y walks into the silver-clad room. When the entrance closes, I can hear faint talking on the other side.

I jump with the sudden sound of the cabin door opening, blasting into my ears. I turn to see Zarn walking toward me. His masculine chest and shiny silver pants shine in the white light.

"We're approaching the Hi-Tem circle of worlds," he says to me. I hold my head up, and he looks at my tear-streaked face. "Look, I'm sorry for what Lanzion did. But it-"

"I don't want to talk about it," I say, holding a hand toward him. "Just tell me when we land somewhere."

"We're going to refuel on Stalis Station," Zarn responds. "If you want to relax in some snow, Stalis is right next to Talvir. I heard the planet looks like a face from above."

"I'll just stay on the ship," I respond back.

"Where's 8088-Y?" Zarn asks. I point over to the other door.

"He's in th-"

I'm cut off as a boom shakes the C15, and it flips upside down. Zarn and I crash against the ceiling, and the beds almost land on us. My face smashes against the steel; blood squirting from my nose. The white lights flash red as a deafening siren blasts through the room.

"What happened?" Zarn yells over the noise. I look over to see him smashed against the cockpit door. I reach an arm out to try to crawl over, but the door opens, and I see Lanzion emerge from the other side. He grabs onto Zarn's shoulders, who screams from the suddenness, and is pulled into the main cabin. Lanzion looks back at me for a moment, our eyes locking, and he doesn't hesitate as he steps back into the cockpit. The door closes, and I hear the consoles through the wall.

"Approaching the atmosphere," a female robotic voice says. "Engage emergency breaks or prepare for a sudden crash."

"THE BRAKES ARE GONE!" I hear Zarn yell from beyond the door. I rest my entire body, hopeless to make it through the crash. The C15 begins to violently rumble as it breaks through into the sky of Stalis.

"Fuck you, Lanzion," I whisper as I close my eyes and rest my head against the ceiling, which begins to rise with heat. "Reez, here I come."

—

As the C15 makes contact with the Stalis dirt, I'm thrust down onto the ship's floor. One of my arms folds backward, and my head cracks against the metal. All of the beds and furniture pummel down around me. I wait on the ground for a bit, waiting for Zarn or Lanzion to walk out and most likely ignore me.

After what feels like hours, I decide to just leave. I roll onto my back, examining my broken arm. I can see the elbow bone poking through the skin, and I grab onto the floppy forearm. I take a deep breath, then I pull it toward me. The bones crack, and I feel a rush of pain through my entire body, but I hold back a scream.

I regain the feeling in my fingers, so I grab onto one of the overturned white beds to pull myself up. I wipe away some blood from my forehead, brushing my thumb against a newly opened wound. I walk over to the door leading to the unknown room, and it doesn't budge. Wires hang down from cracked panels in the ceiling, sparking onto me as I try to slide my fingers into a split in the wall.

I push against the door, and it slowly skids open. On the other side, I'm only met with the fiery remains of a ruined room; the walls wholly destroyed and the floor covered in black sludge. 8088-Y and The Seventh are nowhere to be seen. The dark gray lights of the planet shine down on me, reminding me of Loca when I left it. Seems I can't escape the darkness.

I jump over the demolished walls, hopping onto the muddy black ground of Stalis. The crash left an extensive indent trail through the dirt, and it stretches pretty far into the foggy distance. Surrounding the collision, tall, white-brick buildings cast heavy shadows over me. Then, through a break in the clouds, I can see the planet of Talvir, a snow-white circle with a few dots of light-blue lakes. Kind of like a smiley face.

I slide my fingers down my left arm, opening my map. My palm opens, and the familiar blue light shines, albeit a tad bit glitchy. The map of Stalis pops up, and it's mostly a barren planet full of refuel stations and oil rivers. As I look at the map, a little drop of black goo falls onto my forearm.

"Black sludge, ew," I say, closing my map and wiping it off. It leaves a little stain as it falls off. After hearing what I just said, I realize something. "Black sludge...."

The images Meiv gave me flash through my mind again, but only dripping black sludge, an endless sea of blue water, and a brain in a space of black. No fire and burning this time. Did the blazing image represent Loca? Then they're all planets...and that's the path she meant.

"I gotta get to someone," I say out loud, looking around for any sign of life. "But where?"

Looking back at the ruined D16, I realize that I need to make this journey alone. No Zarn, no Lanzion, not even 8088-Y or The Seventh. I have been winging everything alone this whole time, and only when I'm with someone else does it get fucked up. The only time I've ever felt safe with someone else was with Reez.

Maybe if I follow this trail, I can find a way to reunite with him. I can find a way to stop all of this. Help my own cause and save the seven Gods along the way. I would still love to go to Inaz and have my own little place to grow and sell crops. One day, Janx. One day.

I begin to walk through the valley of brick walls, not knowing where I'm going. But that's the point. I'll just walk until I stumble across a path to an endless sea. Going from a sea of black to a sea of blue. Hopefully.

—

Eventually, the hills and valleys of sludge transform into the light gray concrete of a drop-off center. Large tube-like towers with yellow lights down the sides stretching out into little pads for ships and transports to land on. They line the miles-long area, and each tube seems to have an inside elevator leading down to the bottom level, which is where I stand.

I hurry along the white and gold-plated tile floor, passing by scavengers, traders, and travelers. Despite having only dirty pants on and having to cover my chest with my arms, nobody stares or tries to advance on me. They all seem like pleasant, entertaining people, completely different than the horrific areas I used to be on Loca.

One being catches my eye; someone, or something, adorned in complete pastel yellow and green garments. The colors are almost an escape from everything: black, gray, and orange. He sticks out like a sore thumb, too. I approach him just as he finishes talking to a lengthy Arma-Human, who walks off with a laugh.

"Hey, little lady. Need a jacket?" he says. He removes a light green jacket and hands it to me, to which I slowly grab it from him. "You look beat up. May I treat those?"

"Do you have a ship?" I quickly ask. I drape the jacket over my shoulders, so my arms don't leave my bare chest. "Or just…anything I can be on?"

"Uh, yeah…," the man calmly says. "Are you running from something?"

"I just need to be alone while being able to rest," I respond. "Please."

"Yeah, I have a Hauling Ship model-P-o33 on platform 3B of this tower I lean on," he says. I look up at the gray tower he is, in fact, leaning on, seeing all of the ships fly through the sky. "Just use this and go up there, and I'll join you in a few minutes."

He reaches into a pocket on his pretty yellow pants and hands me a small rectangular card. It's decorated with little flowers and a light blue background. The words 'Imbue Hauling Services' can be read in a slanted, lovely pink color.

"Thank you," I say to him. I quickly rush past him into the opening of the tower. I enter one of the many elevators it has, and the silver interior and white light bring back some images of the D16. "I hope they're alright."

The elevator door closes, sealing me from the black and gray sludge. I look at the wall, where besides my warped reflection, a small slit on the wall beckons for the card.

"Insert card for verification," it says in a male robotic voice. I slide the card into the hole, and a little jingle plays over a speaker system in the ceiling. "Thank you. Enjoy your travels and trades."

The elevator jolts into motion, and it leisurely takes me upward. I slide the card back out and wonder how the man is going to get up if I have his ticket. I look at my reflection, the distorted view of my body seemingly bending straight in my mind. I can see where all my burns were; a little seam outlines where they disappeared from.

I look at my new jacket. It's comfortable, but not Reez's. I love the colors, though; it's gorgeous. I take the opportunity to zip up the jacket, which fits loosely on my slimmer body. As I continue to look at the walls, the moving elevator comes to a slow and relaxing stop. The door opens, and I walk onto one of the landing pads.

A large, bulking light blue square sits atop four stubby landing apparatuses. It rests on the bay, sitting in the dark light. Little yellow spotlights on the edges of the circular pad shine outward into the sky, and I pass by them as I approach the craft. A short staircase leads into the dark-blue lit insides.

"You took a little long to make it this far," the man says from behind me. As I turn, he's already walking past. "Come on, I'll let you tell me everything on the way to Baorealious."

"The trade planet?" I ask, jogging up to him. He stands next to the staircase, motioning for me to go first. I do, and he follows behind. I walk into the main chamber room, where I'm met with a relaxing row of comfortable-looking beds.

"Feel free to use any of those," the man says. "But for now, come to the main consoles."

He walks between the rows of beds over to a silver steel ladder leading up into a ceiling hole. I make my way up behind him, shaking at each hand movement. Passing the hole, I enter a large cabin area, where two oblong crystal clear windows peer out into the dark sky. The light blue walls are lined with computers, buttons, and switches, all blinking different colors. The lighting is a soft yellow, unlike the dark blue down the ladder.

The man takes a seat on a cushiony, laid-back purple chair, which is seated right next to another one, this one empty. He clicks and clacks some things on the consoles, and I feel the ship shake. Outside, I can see the environment sink down. We are flying.

"Take a seat. It'll last longer," he says. I do just that; sitting down on the empty chair. "So, ma'am. Tell me. What's got you in a hurry on Stalis?"

"I'm running from death and toward it simultaneously," I respond. "Does that make sense?"

"Too much."

~The Note~

I take Reez's notebook from my back pocket, thanking fate that I didn't leave it in the jacket. Flipping through the pages, I see sketches of odd creatures I've never seen. Beings from Earth I & II, the many Loca moons, and even the deepest colonies of Inaz. But one page stands out; the very last one.

Taped to the final yellow, slightly brown-stained page, a crumbled note flows in the wind. I pull on the edge, tearing the plastic tape clean off. I close the book, sliding it back into my pocket and trying my best to straighten the note. I can see Reez's large, scribbled signature written in heavy black ink on the bottom, underneath a plethora of words.

'Janx, my beloved adventurer,

You have always been on my mind ever since we met on the beach of Stoean. The night that we watched the bombs, they set off midair…letting the colors shine across our faces. If I could have that night happen again, I'd give all I have.

I really do wish we could have been together. Trust me, I wanted you all to myself since that night. But I let the hatred I have for everything else blind me. Yet, you were always my light. Now, of course, if you're reading this, then I am long dead. I hope you didn't have to watch it happen.

I want you to ensure that everything you do to help this universe is done for everyone else. Not me. I only want you to think about me when you are at your lowest points. The nights of regrets, the sad storms, and the depressive episodes. Remember the good times we had together.

I know that one day we will meet again, whether in another life or whatever awaits us after death. I am already there, waiting for you in open arms and an open heart. You never left my thoughts, Janx. When you dream at night, think about what could happen if you could rewrite our story.

I'm writing this note while in the back rooms of Prince Gewarsh's whore house. If these are my last moments, just know I used them all thinking about you. I love you too.

-Reez'

I hold the note in my hands, watching as droplets of tears stain between the words. I reread it over and over, wishing everything could've been different. I carefully fold the note into a small square, putting it in my back pocket next to the book. I quickly glance around the light blue transport vehicle's walls around me. Then, I close my eyes and interlock my fingers, leaning my head against my hands.

"Can you hear me?" I ask aloud. "You probably can't. I'm just talking to myself, but I can feel you with me every moment. I just wish it was physical…instead of spiritual. I wish I died instead of you. You didn't deserve any of this.

Could I trade this life for one that involves just you? I'll search the ends of the universe to find a way. I promise you, Ree. I cross my beaten heart, and I hope to die if there is genuinely no way. Maybe then I'll be back with you."

Something hits the outside of the vehicle, which rocks it forward and knocks me out of my thoughts. All I have to do is find what the 'water' part of my travel means…then maybe I can understand what Meiv sent me to do. But for now, I'm trapped in a thought prison of Reez, and all that has transpired on Loca.

~The Seventh~

The area around me lights up with white light; the first light I have seen since I was wished away. Drops of snow land on my moss-colored shell of a body. I look down at my hands; ten thin, barbed fingers feeling the soft touch of the white flakes from the sky. I try to feel for my legs, but they don't react. From under the blanket of white, I can see my torn limbs disappear under the bleached ground, with only the stains of age remaining on the snow.

I blink my vibrating eyes a few times; the snow falls through my decaying husk. The clouds above darken ever so slightly as a shadow trudges to me from my right. The person leans down and looks at me, and they light up a small match by brushing it against their chest. The light brightens their face, and I see a Commission Stalker.

A face encased in half of a metal mask, with a thin curved green visor across the shining blood-red steel. His exposed lower turquoise skin overlaps itself with bulging wrinkles and rashes. A little antenna on the left side of his mask beeps with a blinking red light at the top of the pole. I can see little waves of dispersing energy as the beeps bring in unknown signals.

The rest of his body is warped, unlike anything I've ever seen. A swollen neck leads into light-green, and pink cloth draped over a skeletal body, five lengthy arms, and two triple-jointed legs. As I look up into his blinding visor, the snow around us continues to fall from the blank gray sky.

"Good evening. You took quite a tumble; I could feel you fall from across the goddamn Watcher's Trail," he says. "Your energy levels are off the charts...the antennae is how I can tell."

"Who...are you?" I ask. The man puts his arms under me and pulls me up. I rest on my legless crotch. "Where am I?"

"I am The Eternal Brian; overseer of the known universe," he says. He sits down next to me on a mound of snow, putting his arms across his knees. "I'm on a bit of a mission at the moment...searching for any high energy readings. I was on Inaz when I could sense a sudden spike in Entity Energy, so I ran over."

"Ran? How'd you run from Inaz to...here?" I ask.

"Well, I can't run, but I can open gateways between points," Brian explains. "If you tell me where you came from, I can send you back."

"Gateways?" I ask. I can do that...how can he? "Where do you pull the power from?"

"I can pull energy from anything...and Earth II is a big commodity for reusing it. I can pull as much power from Earth II as I want because I can crush the energy down by wasting it all on one or two gateways," Brian says. "So yeah, who are you, and where do you need to go?"

"My name is The Seventh, and I was on Roan the last time I was...awake," I say. Brian tilts his head.

"You're one of the seven gods?" he asks in confusion. "That's why your levels are so high...but you can't be the reason...."

"The reason for what?" I ask.

"Look, I shouldn't be saying this, but...this universe's energy levels are spiking. Too much is being let out to stroll around the galaxy. It's in danger of fracturing The Eternal Brain," he says. "You'll have to come with me, now."

"Why?" I ask.

"Well," Brian laughs. "You need new legs, and I can't get confused for you again. Stay by my side so my antennae can rebalance."

"I guess I have no choice. I need to find out how I was brought back as well...," I say.

"Mr. Seventh?" something asks. I look up to see some sort of thin, humanoid light blue android stumbling through the high snow. "If you don't mind, I am 8088-Y, and I accompanied you on your fall down. I believe this is yours?"

The robot holds out a cracked glass jar with a thrashing blue light inside. I quickly push myself up with my hands, grabbing the pot as I fall back to the ground. Brian stands up and stands next to 8088-Y.

"The fuck are you?" he asks. "Didn't know they make your kind so...feminine."

"I am one of Row-N's Leathean Machines; model-C8e," 8088-Y responds. "Codenamed 8088-Y, which is the manufacture number and the generation of model-C8e I was made during."

"I also didn't know they made you all so...talkative," Brian says. 8088-Y puts his hands on his hips and shakes his head.

"I'm coming along with you two because I'm not risking all the rust from the melting snow," 8088-Y says.

"Melting?" Brian and I both ask, looking at 8088-Y with confused expressions. 8088-Y nods.

"Yes, melting," he says. "You can't feel it?"

"No...," I whisper. Brian shrugs and places his hands together. He pushes them as they light up with yellow light. Cracks of lightning shoot out a few feet out, forming together to create a rectangle gateway.

"This...is what... we'll use...to get off here...," Brian strains to say as the doorway forms into a lopsided square of smoky yellow and orange light. When it's finished, he collapses and groans.

"Are you ok?" I ask, placing the jar onto the snow and pulling myself to Brian.

"Yes...yes," he stutters. "Longer distance traveling takes a bit more out of me."

"Look," I sternly say, pointing a crusty green finger in his face. "I'll do the portal openings after this. I can handle it."

"Who are you three?" a fourth voice calls out. I turn only my head to see a half cyborg, half-human hybrid walking through the gateway. A buff chest almost rips through a greasy white shirt he wears. Both arms end at the shoulders in wire-covered stumps, but both have thin metal plates connecting to robotic arms wrapped in human veins. His beefy chest leads up to an equally wide neck, and sitting atop it: is a dark-skinned, plump face with curly black hair. A confused frown leaves his circular yellow eyes wide open.

"Who are YOU is the more important question," I ask, quickly pushing the jar behind me.

"The names Dharall, and you're blocking the entrance to my shop," the man quickly explains. "I have customers…some natives from Loca."

"Is one of them wearing SVE equipment and just crashed near you?" 8088-Y asks. Dharall raises an eyebrow in suspicion and nods. "That's my friends…Janx, Zarn, and Lanzion!"

"They're being questioned in the back of my shop. So get going and join them and close this fucking portal," Dharall complains. Brian picks me up under my armpits and carries me through the gateway, and 8088-Y joins behind. While passing through the doorway, the yellow and orange lights wrap around us, mixing and contorting until they fade into the room of a greasy fuel station.

Dirty shelves and tool-ridden benches line the brown concrete walls, and black sludge leaks down from the cracks in the ceiling. The floor is nonexistent; we find ourselves standing on squishy black dirt. Cracked, smudged bay windows peer out into a black cloud sky, with mounds of dark liquid dripping from it. Void-colored mountains and inky rivers border the distant land.

In the middle of the current room sits a blue-gray steel table, which Brian sets me down on. Dharall leans against a tall red press, looking out through the windows. 8088-Y searches through a cardboard box of scraps in a far corner as Brian tells him what to look for.

"Hold on, you think you can just use my shit? I let you come back here to find your friends," Dharall says, walking over to Brian. He grabs onto Brian's shoulder, spinning him around.

"Shut your shithole," Brian says, covering Dharall's mouth with one of his five hands. "We need to get that guy legs, and I don't see you helping."

Dharall grabs Brian's arm and pulls it away from his face.

"If you needed legs, just say that. I thought he was born that way. Hell, my species is," Dharall exclaims. He walks back to the press, pulling down a black lever on its side. "I have tons. All of us Pocomels need to make our own limbs. I'm talking arms, legs, and even balls."

"You have one that can fit his thinner build?" Brian asks, pointing at me. Dharall shrugs.

"Yeah, probably," he responds. A panel in the ceiling opens up, and a rack of metal legs like Dharall's drops down. "If not, I can make it work."

"What's the procedure like?" I ask.

"I'll put you under for a while, and I'll just connect the legs to your neural network," Dharall explains like it's simple.

"Huh?" I ask.

"Your brain," Dharall snaps back. "I'll have to cover your body with some material to keep anything from leaking out, such as your organs. I think that green husk around you is attracting some unwanted visitors."

As he says that, a little bug flies around my torso. It lands on my left shoulder, and I smash my head on it.

"Right...," Dharall says. He flips through the legs and chooses one after four or five. "This one will do."

"How will you put me under?" I ask.

"Simple," Dharall responds. "Like this."

He suddenly uppercuts into my lower jaw, which knocks into my head and blacks my vision out completely.

—

When I awake, I can sense a new feeling below my hips. I can move my newfound legs; big blocky gray limbs creak with each movement. I spin around and jump onto the ground, my body shaking as I land on the dirt. I reach my arms out to balance myself as I try to walk again. At first, it's awkward; the legs being too new and the weight being much heavier than my old ones.

I stumble over to a chipped green wooden door, pushing it open to reveal some sort of bathroom. Brown stains cover the white tiled walls, and the bowl of a toilet is completely smashed; pieces lining the dirt ground. I hold the wall to help with the balance as I feel the touch of sharp glass. Looking to my right, I see my reflection through a shattered mirror.

My green husk of a body is wrapped with protective brown bags, stitched together with light blue rope. The cloth over my chest ends in ripped edges above my waist, and I can see my loose intestines underneath. The fabric over my head only shows my deep, cloudy gray eyes and toothy mouth. I place both hands on the mirror, and I see the barbed joints, and my mind flashes with memories, ones I remember but can't make out. Images of a woman…some sort of city…and a wrinkled gray man.

The flashes become too much, and my head begins to hurt. I grab the bag over my face, ripping and tearing it off. After the deed is done, I look down and pull at the fabric over my torso. Then, I throw the pieces onto the ground and look back at my face.

I notice the crusty green plastic around my body is gone, and my peachy natural body is all that's left. My head is all but a clammy orb of flesh, a crack down the middle that leaks flowing purple light. My droopy cloudy eyes and unclosable mouth remain the same as I saw them before.

As for my torso, some of the green husk still supports my frame, but most of it in the front is gone. All that's left is the maze of pink intestines and organs that is hardly covered by the shredded brown cloth. I look back at my fingers, and the images begin flashing again. My face pulses even more; the pain being around the hole on my head.

I slam my fingers against the bare wall opposite the mirror. I grab at my hands and tear the wire off, which brings some peachy skin along with it. I continue to peel and rip until my fingers are all but bones protruding from bleeding shredded palms.

"We're catching up with the others. One of our group isn't here, however. Is everything ok?" 8088-Y asks from beside me. His sudden appearance makes me jump.

"Yes, yes," I stutter out. All my words and actions are very jittery and sudden. "Just…trying not to remember."

"Trying not to remember who you are?" 8088-Y asks. "We need you to do that."

"Yes, but every time I try, all I can feel is negative energy," I respond. "I don't think someone like you would know what feelings are like."

"Well…," 8088-Y says in a lower, softer voice. "You would be surprised with what I can do."

With that, he walks out of the bathroom and out of view. Shortly after, I walk out of the bathroom as well, through the room where I was worked on, and out into a courtyard surrounded by colossal white brick walls. Inky black liquids drip from the tops of the barriers; the light gray skies leak a similar fluid. I meet up with 8088-Y and some others in the middle of the broad clearing, introducing myself to some new allies.

"Lanzion and Zarn…both from the same planet?" I ask, shaking hands with the two of them. Although they both hesitate, I can sense they mean well.

"No, I'm the governor of the entire Termehus system, besides the planet of Treenun… there are a few broken peace treaties between Treenun's government and

I," Zarn explains. "And Lanzion here is just a scavenger from Tubhadphrik city. It's a place on Inaz."

"An Inaz boy, huh?" I jokingly say. "Didn't know farmers knew how to build civilizations as well."

"Listen here," Lanzion says, shoving past Zarn and pointing a finger into my face. "I don't know how Inaz was when YOU were around, but farming is why most people move there."

"Lanzion, calm down; he's just an old-timer," Zarn says, trying to pull Lanzion back. "Let's go find Janx."

"She probably already left...at this point, we should just dump this guy here and find a new D16," Lanzion yells, pushing Zarn off him. "Or maybe The Seventh bitch can cough up a few sugola coins for an E17-Visor Mat."

"Hey, you two," The Eternal Brian cuts in, standing between Lanzion and me. He points at the two boys. "I don't need you two. But I need The Seventh, and we're going to continue our search with or without you two."

"Well, I certainly don't want to stay here...so I'll go with them," 8088-Y says, wiping some sludge off his chest. "And maybe he can get us an E17, and we can travel faster."

"So we're just going to search for some energy, huh?" Lanzion complains. "And your little rod will beep when we find some?"

"How much did you tell them?" I ask Brian.

"All of it. They need to know...especially since we need more in our group. The amounts of energy in the base

215

levels are even rising…and this is NOT normal," Brian explains. "I mean if they don't come with us…then what will they go do?"

"Fine," Zarn agrees. "We'll go find your energy spike. Is it pointing you in any direction?"

"I've been traveling out from The Eternal Brain…and even though this planet borders the Unknown Advances, the levels are still low. Whatever this spike is… it's not close."

As Brian explains his journey up until he found me, a rock rolls into my foot. I look down, seeing the small gray ball rest against my fleshly heel. A whispering rings through my ears, and the voice of Brian and the others fade out of range. I follow the path of the rock back to one of the white walls, walking through a slight crack within the stones.

I squeeze through, shuffling past wooden boards and the back of peeling wallpaper, shambling between the buildings' walls. On the other side, I pop out into a sand-colored brick chamber, where I see a black hooded figure in the doorway across from me. Orange light from beyond him flows across the walls, wrapping around my fleshy body.

"Excuse me?" I ask. The figure lifts its arms, delicate snow-white fingers pulling at the hood. It's brought down, and so is the rest of the robe. It falls to the ground, and a sudden wind blows it against my legs. I look at the revealed body, seeing a woman's bare back.

Lengthy black hair trickles down bony white skin, ending above the spherical, shiny ass. Her legs crisscross each other, and they're covered with knee-high black boots. She slowly wipes her hands down her sides, ceasing the movements once her fingers wrap around her hips. She spins her body around with her legs, and the sand-colored walls bleed with black. I look at her front, but my vision blurs around her body. I can faintly make out her features, but my eyes begin quivering as I squint them.

"Who are you?" I ask as she reaches an arm out. I step forward, holding my hand out, and right before our fingers touch, I'm pulled along by a sudden force.

"Wake the fuck up, man!" Lanzion yells in my face, holding onto my arm. I sporadically blink, violently thrashing my head around to examine my surroundings. I find myself back in the courtyard with the others and slowly retrieve my sense of feeling. Lanzion lets go, and my arm drops down to my side.

"You were in some sort of trance," he says. "But let's go, Brian scored an H19-Oral Bumfuzzle, and we're about to travel to Earth I."

"Ok, right, right," I say, looking back to the white stone wall; now a crackless barrier.

"I asked him why he couldn't portal us there, and he said that would mess with his readings," Lanzion continues. "Anyway, let's go meet up with him."

"Right...right," I say, slowly walking forward, not taking my eyes off the wall. A quick image of the woman flashes in my head, but I blink it away. Who was that?

Everything about the room seemed so familiar...have I been there before? I doubt it.

~Loca Creature Log~

-Dated: 2038

• Arachnavoids

-Species that have human-like builds, with two large eyes and six smaller ones. Their skin can be gray, brown, black, or white and they grow little hairs that protect them from harmful weather conditions. Two sharp fangs hang on either side of their mouth. Arachnavoids have the ability to grow human hair, in any way or style they want.

-Usual Height: 5-6 Feet Tall

-Usual Weight: 120-135 Pounds

-Danger Level: Low

-Place of Origin: Loca

-Cross-Breed: Yes

• Arma-Human

-Normal humans with varying degrees of yellow skin, due to a condition in which too much bilirubin is created from their blood cells mutating from the Locanagwan water.

-Usual Height: 6-7.5 Feet Tall

-Usual Weight: 140-165 Pounds

-Danger Level: Moderately Low

-Place of Origin: Earth II

-Cross-Breed: Yes

• Ascended Guards

-Large wooden skeletons that connect with the darkest depths of the fiery pits of the universe. Black bones drip lava onto the ground, past their floating upper bodies.

Their bodies are very sharp, due to their higher status as the guards of The Divine's pit.

-Usual Height: 8 Feet Tall
-Usual Weight: 400 Pounds
-Danger Level: Moderate
-Place of Origin: Magona
-Cross-Breed: No

- ## Ascended Priest

-A bony creature of unknown origin. Formed from the four Ascended Guards of Loca during the confrontation with Al-X. He wears an inverted white metal suit that covers his red bones. Spikes adorn his shoulders, and his face is usually seen covered in blood and decorated with mounds of flesh.

-Usual Height: 8.5 Feet Tall
-Usual Weight: Unknown
-Danger Level: Extremely High
-Place of Origin: Loca
-Cross-Breed: No

- ## Ascending Guards

-Large wooden skeletons that connect with nature in order to live. They serve under the Temple of Akur on each planet; serving as the base-line guards. They wear white and purple cloth over their frames. Usually adorned with plants.

-Usual Height: 8 Feet Tall
-Usual Weight: 320 Pounds
-Danger Level: Extremely Low

-Place of Origin: Magona
-Cross-Breed: No

• Barbarians

-Warriors from a forgotten time. They waltz around in small clothing, usually only sporting a few pieces of fabric over their goods. Barbarians are known for their heavy muscles, extensive egos, and overgrown hair.
-Usual Height: 6-7 Feet Tall
-Usual Weight: 130-165 Pounds
-Danger Level: Moderate
-Place of Origin: Vhorlarx
-Cross-Breed: No

• Bo-Telail

-Underwater medics bred to care for each other, since they usually live alone. Their brain is surrounded by an almost translucent chamber of steel, that sits in the top of their tentacle-covered neon faces. Their eyes are nothing but dark black orbs, with a small white circle on either one. They have no legs, and use fins and a tail to move around.
-Usual Height: 4-5 Feet Tall
-Usual Weight: 50-75 Pounds
-Danger Level: Extremely Low
-Place of Origin: Unknown
-Cross-Breed: No

• Canilupus

-Tall, Felishe-like creatures that have snout-like noses, tall floppy ears, and sharp fangs. Their bodies are covered in small hairs that are used to aid their complex touch sense.

They're usually trained for combat from birth, and unlike Felishes, are not a cross-bred race.

-Usual Height: 6-7 Feet Tall

-Usual Weight: 135-155 Pounds

-Danger Level: Moderate

-Place of Origin: Canilue

-Cross-Breed: No

- ## Cobbles

-Creatures made from solid rock. Most of the time, they just take relaxing vacations on rock-heavy planets. They give GREAT hugs.

-Usual Height: 6-7 Feet Tall

-Usual Weight: 500-700 Pounds

-Danger Level: Low (When Not Disturbed)

-Place of Origin: Solidified Foremes

-Cross-Breed: No

- ## Creeschuns

-Tall necked, stubby bodied, nerds that excel in boring people to death. They're usually librarians, tour guides, or informational bodies. They traveled to Loca after their home planet, Rhukers, was taken over by Trhools. Dhamaneek was the last living Creeschun until Al-X took his life during the Temple of Akur massacre.

-Usual Height: 8 Feet Tall

-Usual Weight: 50-145 Pounds

-Danger Level: Extremely Low

-Place of Origin: Rhukers

-Cross-Breed: Yes

• DemiGods

-Currently, seven DemiGods are known to exist. So far, only Janx and Tyre have been identified as one.
-Usual Height: Unknown
-Usual Weight: Unknown
-Danger Level: Possibly High
-Place of Origin: The Seventh
-Cross-Breed: No

• Devil-Fetus

-The in-progress parasite to infect Al-X, taken too early, and resulted in the unkillable child of the Netherworld. An armless, soulless, motherless, baby that has a taste for spines.
-Usual Height: 2-3 Feet Tall
-Usual Weight: 20-35 Pounds
-Danger Level: Extremely High
-Place of Origin: Juwles
-Cross-Breed: No

• Dice Bots

-Al-X's casino guards; created from scraps left over from the Mechanical Carishem Revolution. Row-N hates the build of the Dice Bots, since they are very unstable and can't aid in anything but decoration. Al-X says Row-N is full of his own shit.
-Usual Height: 5-5.5 Feet Tall
-Usual Weight: 300-325 Pounds
-Danger Level: Low
-Place of Origin: Al-X

-Cross-Breed: No

• Felishe

-Furry humans with small noses, ears on the top of their heads, and eyes with thin pupils. Their hair can be any shade of brown, black, or white and they usually wear clothes that match it. Their eyes are sought after presents for little children on Inaz, since they are almost like a good luck charm. Felishes hate children, even their own, because of this.
-Usual Height: 7 Feet Tall
-Usual Weight: 115-120 Pounds
-Danger Level: Moderate
-Place of Origin: Earth II
-Cross-Breed: Yes

• Foremes

-Made from the gas of the Infinite Flames; a section of negative energy light years away that can create sentient, forever burning beings. They can take the parts of other beings in order to use them for themselves.
-Usual Height: 9-12 Feet Tall
-Usual Weight: 0 Pounds
-Danger Level: Extremely High
-Place of Origin: Infinite Flames
-Cross-Breed: No

• Formics

-Bug faced humans that usually cover their deformities with cloaks, hoods, and masks. They have large quantities of hair on their heads, which can come in any neon color.

It matches their usually brightly colored skin, complete with silver eyes. Their bodies bulge with blood-heavy veins, and their mouths sit between two hairy pincers.

-Usual Height: 6-7 Feet Tall

-Usual Weight: 135-139 Pounds

-Danger Level: Moderately High

-Place of Origin: Formos

-Cross-Breed: Yes

• Humans

-Almost 97% of the time, humans are ranked among the worst possible species, the most boring, and the most likely to abuse your race. More people were happy then afraid when Earth II was destroyed, only because they thought it was the natural death of the planet. Humans are the main reason that Magona's plan exists, since they are the reason for most of the cross-bred species alive.

-Usual Height: 5-6 Feet Tall

-Usual Weight: 136 Pounds

-Danger Level: Non-existent

-Place of Origin: Earth I

-Cross-Breed: No

• Infrens

-Fiery beings that are the top cause of deforestation, house fires, and arson. Their hearts beat with the heat of 10,000°, which could boil someone's skin with a single touch. They're usually bright orange in color, and while most have been killed, some still roam the lands of beautiful worlds, wanting to turn it black and red.

-Usual Height: 5-6 Feet Tall

-Usual Weight: 150-175 Pounds

-Danger Level: High

-Place of Origin: The Netherworld

-Cross-Breed: No

• Kuroledies

-Beautiful beings that were the first species to be wiped out by Magona. There were only around 100 when he began his plan when he saw The Seventh fall in love with one. Now, The Seventh is haunted with the image of 100 graves dotting the barren Sarion grounds, and the memory of his Kuroledy taken from him.

-Usual Height: 4-6 Feet Tall

-Usual Weight: 75-100 Pounds

-Danger Level: Low

-Place of Origin: Sarion

-Cross-Breed: Yes

• Marajuanians

-Unbreakable wooden frames akin to a human skeleton, covered in grass and leaves. Their heart burns for eternity, and it burns the green, causing the surrounding people to sniff the fumes and can possibly go through psychedelic experiences. Ten out of ten scavengers recommend having a Marajuanian on your trip.

-Usual Height: 5.5-6 Feet Tall

-Usual Weight: 85-115 Pounds

-Danger Level: Extremely Low

-Place of Origin: Maraju

-Cross-Breed: No

• Mushrumians

-A native mushroom-headed species, coming from the lost planet of Mushrumia. They live in the caves of the samely-named Mushrumia, near the Province of Stoean's mining colony. Their bodies are usually featureless, white or gray blobs that they hop around on, and their heads are large mushroom tops with varying patterns. They do not have eyes, so they use vibrations to see, nor do they have mouths. They communicate only in the ancient Mushrumian language.

-Usual Height: 10 Feet Tall

-Usual Weight: 50-75 Pounds

-Danger Level: Extremely Low

-Place of Origin: Mushrumia (Planet)

-Cross-Breed: Yes

• Nag-Souls

-A silhouette of humans that is made of negative energy, which reverses gravity within its body. This causes the Nag-Souls to be a mirror of everything around it, but reflects everything in monotone, and in backwards order. Nag-Souls are used to show someone's future, but once seen, it cannot be changed. They are outlawed from entering any Cosmo-Edge ring planets.

-Usual Height: 5-6 Feet Tall

-Usual Weight: Reverses gravity inside its body

-Danger Level: High

-Place of Origin: Time

-Cross-Breed: No

• Orugnics

-Only a few Orugnics have been seen in the wild. Most decide to stay on their untouchable Cosmo-Edge ring planet of Orugno. Marz is one such traveler, and he represents the white-haired elders. Most Orugnics are fighters, trying to save their planet from the political corruption of the Treenun ring.

-Usual Height: 3-5 Feet Tall

-Usual Weight: 45-65 Pounds

-Danger Level: Moderately Low

-Place of Origin: Orugno

-Cross-Breed: Yes

• Phroug

-Tall, but bent creatures with an upside-down arch shape. Their legs connect at the top to the body, and large white eyes are embedded into their flesh. The feet are blocky stones that are compiled of bundled dead skin from humans, usually. They're popular among billboard hangers, shooting ranges, and clubs, for some reason.

-Usual Height: 6 Feet Tall

-Usual Weight: 80-85 Pounds

-Danger Level: Moderate

-Place of Origin: Earth I

-Cross-Breed: Yes

- # Pocomels

-Humans that traveled to Pocomel, and somehow evolved to become armless and legless. They must train with their upper body and mouth in order to create their own limbs. This causes most Pocomels to have chests as large as a doorframe, and a chin as sharp as a knife. They have since become one of the most intelligent races.

-Usual Height: 2-3 Feet Tall

-Usual Weight: 55-80 Pounds

-Danger Level: Low

-Place of Origin: Pocomel

-Cross-Breed: Yes

- # Pēchaucks

-Elegant, stubby flyers with long necks, small heads, and skinny arms. Their legs are also slender, with four small toe-like bones poking out from the bottom. Their bodies are just circles decorated with colorful hairs that extrude with large feathers, acting as a symbol of their wisdom. They are usually hated for being extremely annoying and hypocritical.

-Usual Height: 3-5 Feet Tall

-Usual Weight: 70-90 Pounds

-Danger Level: Low

-Place of Origin: Loca

-Cross-Breed: Yes

• Row-N's Leathean Machines

-The genius inventions from one Row-N. Machines built to help the construction of new towns and cities across Loca, and also aid in the findings of new medical practices. During the Magona takeover, Row-N perfected the body of his machines, but still stayed in his favorite model-A99 all his life.

-Usual Height: 8-10 Feet Tall
-Usual Weight: 1-2 Tons
-Danger Level: All
-Place of Origin: Row-N
-Cross-Breed: No

• The Divine

-Magona's original plan to start over. The Divine of every inhabited planet still remains, even Loca's. To the eye of mortals, The Divine is a ball of light akin to the sun. But to the view of DemiGods or those on the brink of death, its true appearance will be seen.

-Usual Height: Unknown
-Usual Weight: Unknown
-Danger Level: High
-Place of Origin: Magona
-Cross-Breed: No

• The Sacred

-The Divine's attempt to create a being that would scare away the population of a planet. After finding out that most species are worse than The Divine thought, it usually gave up and fell into a deep sleep. However, Loca's

Sacred, Al-X, was subject to a lot of development as his own person, instead of being a puppet.

-Usual Height: Unknown

-Usual Weight: Unknown

-Danger Level: High

-Place of Origin: The Divine

-Cross-Breed: No

- ## Travish

-Buck tooth, big-eyed humans with dark colored skin. Their bodies are always moist, and they have large slits that connect to their lungs, allowing them to breathe above water. Their bodies are also decorated with tribal tattoos, since Travishes are very keen on keeping their roots close.

-Usual Height: 3-5 Feet Tall

-Usual Weight: 250-300 Pounds

-Danger Level: Low

-Place of Origin: Wastro

-Cross-Breed: Yes

- ## Varmpur

-A forest predator with sharp teeth and an unquenchable thirst for blood. They usually have big builds, dark skin, bald heads, and an unkillable smile that reveals their sharp incisors. They usually hide in the tall Tranzle forests, where they fall atop their prey. Despite their fierce appearance, most do not know how to fight, and carry floppy swords that appear like serrated steel ones.

-Usual Height: 6-7 Feet Tall

-Usual Weight: 150-200 Pounds

-Danger Level: Moderately High
-Place of Origin: Tranzle
-Cross-Breed: Yes

• Zargon

-Zargons are creatures that share similarities to most Earth II stories of dragons and reptiles. They have scales for skin, large horns on their heads, and an appetite for humans. All non-human species don't fear Zargons, but even beings with 1% human DNA are horrified when they see one. Zargons have the largest count for discrimination on Loca, and the highest amount of murders are of Zargons.
-Usual Height: 6-9 Feet Tall
-Usual Weight: 300-500 Pounds
-Danger Level: Dangerous
-Place of Origin: Zargo
-Cross-Breed: No

• Zhalk's Species

-Although most of this species is unknown, all that can be agreed upon is their five-armed bodies and creative clothing choices.
-Usual Height: Unknown
-Usual Weight: Unknown
-Danger Level: Unknown
-Place of Origin: Unknown
-Cross-Breed: Unknown

~The Order of The Universe~

• The Eternal Brain

-The very middle of the known universe and the center point for every universe that has and will ever exist. It binds all of time and space together and needs to be watched over.

-0 Planet Groups

-Known Planets: The Eternal Brain

• Brain Ring

-The ring of planets that borders The Eternal Brain. A lot of smaller, more compact planets and civilizations. The most common religion amongst the inhabitants is a changed version of Sevrinchístt, where they believe The Eternal Brain to be their one true God.

-4 Planet Groups

-Known Planets: Vecimt, Cöpar

• Mesial Ring

-Despite having fewer groups than the Churle Ring, the Mesial Ring is the most popular of them all. Roan used to be the most populated planet until the fall, and then Inaz took its spot until the Great Plummet of the economy, then Earth II took its spot until 2036, and now Loca is first for population.

-7 Planet Groups

-Known Planets: Earth II, Loca, Inaz, Roan

• Churle Ring

-The ring with the most, yet with the least. The Churle
Ring has around 634 planets, yet only 4 of them are
inhabitable. Most of the Churle Ring is clogged with
Formes gasses that were left unchecked around the time
Magona was banished.
-12 Planet Groups
-Known Planets: Jouruesa

• Astrual Ring

-The Astrual ring is the home of planets most people wish
not to visit. The Valley is closed off to most, Earth I has a
troubling history, and the other planets are just as
suspicious.
-10 Planet Groups
-Known Planets: The Valley, Earth I

• Hi-Tem Ring

-A ring of mostly washed up, tourist planets. The biggest
hub for trading, hunting, gambling, and anything that
groups can get together for. Also home to the universe's
favorite refuel spot: Stalis Station.
-5 Planet Groups
-Known Planets: Talvir, Stalis

Cosmo-Edge Rings

-A ring that is made up of smaller rings of planets that borders the Cosmo barrier. Mostly advanced civilizations that have never traveled beyond the Hi-Tem ring.

-7 Rings, ~4 Planet Groups per Ring

-Known Rings:

–Fivtie Ring

–Known Fivtie Ring Planets: Beriackhayv, Crieyath

Cosmo Field

-A field that borders the universe of nothing. A void absent of anything, it even lacks nothingness. No explorer has dared to cross the Cosmo barrier, but maybe one day someone will.

-0 Planet Groups

-Known Planets: 0